Developmental Editing by Made 4 This Publishing (made4thispublishing@gmail.com)

Copy Editing by Precise Editing Services (www.preciseeditingservices.com)

Book Cover by Sean D. Young

ISBN (paperback): 9798218047115

*NEWS CREDIT: Veronica Meadows— FOX 2 NEWS and Natasha Dado—*Click on Detroit*

Join our virtual book club: EyeCU Reading & Chatting
https://www.facebook.com/groups/670686289760084/?ref=share_group_link

Follow Author Ebony on FB:
https://www.facebook.com/Author-Ebony-Evans-101181896043076/

Follow EyeCU Reading's fan page: EyeCU Reading & Social Network
https://www.facebook.com/profile.php?id=100063715056766

IG: eyecu_ reading
https://instagram.com/eyecu_reading?igshid=YmMyMTA2M2Y=

DEAD TO ME

BY EBONY EVANS

This book is dedicated to my father for reminding me of my talent and inspiring me to write my dreams. Although you are no longer here in body, your presence lives on in my dreams. My dreams know you well. You visit them often. It was your visits that gave me the vision and words to write. I love you, Daddy. I miss your infectious energy and your beautiful smile. Until our next selfie, I look forward to seeing you in my dreams.

My husband, boyfriend, my forever love, confidant, and personal comedian Michael. You are my rock. Thank you for your support and encouragement to use my writing as therapy and healing. Thank you for praying with me and for me. Thank you for being my protector and my provider. Thank you for loving me as I am, spoiling me, and keeping a smile on my face. Thank you for 22 years of marriage. Lord knows it hasn't always been easy, but it's always been worth it. I love you with all that I am.

My daughter Essence. I am so very blessed to be your mother. Every day I look at you in awe and thank God for blessing me with such a beautiful, determined, hardworking, and self-driven young lady. Your existence pushes me to be my best. Everything I do, I do for you.

My angel baby Mychael. I never knew strength until I had you. I am blessed to have had you for 11 months. Coming into the world at a tiny 1lb 4 ounces, you left a huge impact on our hearts. I am the woman I am today because of you.

My best friend Bayyinah. There were very few people who knew I was writing, so thank you for being my sounding board, my rock, and my God-given sister. Thank you for always showing me unconditional love, for being there through the highs and the lows, through the tears and joy. Thank you for showing me that family doesn't always have to be blood. No matter what, I know without a doubt that you will always have my back. Love you to the grave and beyond.

My friend Stacye Lewis, a.k.a. EyeCU Reading's Freestyle Queen. Girl, you make this book writing thing look easy! Thank you for always being down for whatever and inspiring me to put my creativity to use. You've always inspired me and gassed me up. You always told me to just write, and the rest will come. Well, looka here! I was listening. You told me to do it, and I did it!

THANK YOU FOR READING <u>DEAD TO ME</u>. IF YOU ENJOY THIS READ, PLEASE LEAVE A REVIEW AND RECOMMEND TO A FRIEND.

I gave my all

Still they said it wasn’t enough.

I tried to do better

Still they magnified my flaws.

I put others before me

Still they said I was selfish.

I showed them my heart

Still they only saw my past.

I shared my story

Still they ridiculed my mistakes.

I told them my dreams

Still they laughed at my vision.

I gave my life to Christ

Still they pointed out my sins.

But through it all I’ve realized...

I’m here to please God not them.

~ Unknown

"This whole story is completely true, except for all the parts that are totally made up."

-Shonda Rhimes

PROLOGUE

Monday, February 24th, 2020

This is some hot ass chili. Good, but hot. That's what I get for using that Creole recipe. A northerner like me ain't used to all these spices. All I wanted was some chili for this cold day. Now, my nose running, tongue bur—

"Babe! You okay?!"

I ran from the kitchen table and met my husband Charles at the door after he stormed through it. He had just come in from his daily run. He was bent over, clutching his knees, shirt soaking wet. He ran every day. I mean eight days a week. He never sweated that hard. It was also snowing outside. He had no reason to be sweating that hard.

"Charles, did you take a new route? Ran faster than you usually do?" I asked, while running my hands across his face.

His head remained down as he tried to catch his breath. His chest was heaving, his back was rising and falling. I tried to straighten his back out, but he wouldn't budge. I heard him trying to answer me, but words couldn't make their way out of his mouth.

"I'm calling 911. I'm afraid you're having a heart attack."

As I was turning to run to the phone, he grabbed my shirt, stopping me. That's when he looked up at me. I finally saw his face. He wasn't sweating; he was crying. He stood up and exhaled a breath that I could tell he had been holding in a long time. I backed out of his grasp and said nothing.

Charles was not a crier. He kept all of his emotions in check. He was always cool, calm, collected. He kept my world together when it was falling apart.

I was horrified. I couldn't speak! I couldn't ask what was wrong. I was terrified of what he might say. But I was even more terrified to walk away not knowing.

"What's wrong, Charles?" I squeaked.

He stooped down, pressed me against his tears-filled shirt, and whispered, "Ivory, they found him."

Chapter 1

February 14, 2020
DAY 1- Friday

Morning, Goonets. Not sure if you all are aware of the father who's been MIA now close to 24 hours. He's in the truck, but that's all I know. Pray for safe returns is what the text from my brother Curtis, Jr. to me and my sisters Honey and Rihanna read.

Whose father? I texted back.

Curtis, Jr. immediately called me.

"Hello?" I answered the phone.

"You know we ain't heard from Daddy since he left for his appointment earlier yesterday," my brother Curtis, Jr. said.

"Wait. What?" I asked for clarification.

I was washing the dishes when I answered the phone. I put the dishrag down to listen with my full attention. Whenever Curtis, Jr.—CJ for short—called, he was always drunk and on some bullshit, so I usually half paid attention to his conversation. But I was invested this time.

"Girl, we haven't heard from Daddy," he repeated, nonchalantly.

"Since what time yesterday?! And who is we?"

"*We* is me and his wife Jackie. And we both saw him yesterday when he left the house to go to his appointment. He left around ten a.m."

My head darted to the clock on the wall. It was five-thirty in the morning. Almost time for me to leave for work, but that would have to wait.

"So when you say you and his wife haven't heard from him, you mean that y'all have called him?"

"Naw. I mean that we have sent pigeons with notes in their mouths. Yes, Ivory! We been calling him since about two o'clock yesterday. And he hasn't answered."

"That is not like Daddy! Did you check with the hospital to make sure he even made it to his appointment?!"

At this point, I was screaming to the high heavens. My dad lived with his phone in his hand like a Millennial and Gen Z. Half the time, he texted his reply to my text before I even sent it. He was never without his phone. No calls ever went unanswered. I couldn't tell you what his voicemail sounded like because I never heard it.

"Who are you? The FBI? Damn, Ivory. He is a grown ass man who ain't doing nothing but laying up with one of his hoes. You know it's Valentine's Day. He surely don't wanna be getting it from home. I was just telling you so that if and when he calls you, let us know. He's too embarrassed to call me or Jackie back. But he'll call you or Charles."

"I don't know, CJ. I don't have a good feeling about this."

"You never have a good feeling about anything, Ivory. You're just a worry wart who is always looking for a reason to whine. Have a great day. Goodbye."

He hung up the phone before I could ask anything else. He did that shit on purpose. But he was right. Daddy was a hoe. He couldn't even fight it, not that he tried. It just was in his bones, and if he wasn't hoeing, he wasn't being himself.

I tried to go back to washing the residue of breakfast off the dishes, but my mind wouldn't let me be. I knew that CJ was right, but I still had to run it by my best friend. Whenever I burped, I had to tell her. Something like this, I surely had to tell her.

"Que Que! Hey, Girl, hey!"

"Hey, Ivy! You must be calling me to tell me about that dinner I told you to make Charles! I know you hate chicken with bones in it, but wasn't it good? I told you coating it in cornstarch before air frying it would make it the crispiest crunchiest chicken you ever had.

"And I know we're on Weight Watchers, but, Girl! We have to try this pineapple cake with chocolate and roasted pecans. I don't know how many points it is, but I figure if we don't eat nothing else that day, we'll be fine.

"Oh! Guess who I ran into at the store today? Baldheaded Brittany from high school. I know that was almost thirty years ago, but that bitch still don't have nothing but a scoop of hair on her head. She acted like she didn't see me, and I acted like I didn't see her. But she know she saw me!"

"Nobody has heard from my dad in almost twenty-four hours!" I blurted out.

She said nothing for a few seconds. "Huh? Mr. Curtis is missing?"

I nervously laughed, trying to make it seem like no big deal. "Girl. At least that's what he wants us to think. He ain't fooling nobody. Like CJ said, he just laid up with one of his hoes. It got too good to him, and he couldn't get out of it. He's probably sleeping in it."

Que hesitated, "Oookaaayyy. Have *you* tried to call him?"

"No. CJ is right. Like he said, he's just with one of his women."

"Ivory, in all these years, you've never said the words, 'CJ is right', nor have you ever said, 'Curtis, Jr. is right'. Now may not be the time to start. This is serious. Mr. Curtis always answers his phone. He wakes up to answer his phone. He puts God on hold to answer his phone."

"I know. But he's okay."

"Is it that you haven't called him because you are afraid that he won't answer your call, either?"

I took a minute to answer. "Yeah."

"I'll call him. And I'll put you on three-way. Hold on."

God, please. Please let him answer. Please, God. Please.

Que clicked back over once she called him. The line trilled. And trilled. And trilled.

And trilled.

“Hey! Sorry it took me so long to get to the phone.”

“Daddy! Don’t scare—”

“It’s because I’m unavailable. Ha! Gotcha, didn’t I? Leave me a message. I don’t know how to check it, though. Matter of fact, just shoot me a text. I’m not going to check this. Peace!”

My heart traveled up to my throat and down through my pelvis. My knees gave out. I held on to the sink to keep from falling.

“Mr. Curtis. It’s Quantavia. Sweet Pea as you call me. Me and Ivy just checking on you. Just wanted to tell you Happy Valentine’s Day, Sugar Pie! Call one of us back, please. We ain’t gonna fuss at you. I’m lying. You know I will. But Ivory won’t. Love you.”

She hung up the phone.

“Ivy? Ivory?”

I couldn’t speak.

“I’m on my way, Ivory. You’ll just have to be late for work today.”

“No!” I quickly said. “I’ll be fine. Daddy’s fine. Just pray for us.”

I finished up and went to work. I said nothing to no one at work about my daddy missing.

He was going to pop up. No need in getting people in an uproar.

It was Valentine's Day. Charles and I had already celebrated it on Monday because I was off. I am so thankful we did because my mind wasn't focused on being romantic or being romanticized. Curtis Jones —my dad— was all I could think about, whether I admitted it or not.

Chapter 2

February 15, 2020
DAY 2- Saturday

I'm not sure when I went to sleep the night before. Que came over that night. She, my husband, and I stayed up all night, laughing and sharing stories about my daddy. We all knew that he never not answered his phone; we all knew that something was wrong. We just couldn't say it out loud.

As soon as I opened my eyes the next morning, I checked my phone. Nothing from Daddy or anyone telling me they heard from Daddy.

He's not answering anyone's phone call because they're not me. I'm his favorite person in the whole wide world. He'll answer my call.

I called him.

"Hey! Sorry it took me so long to get to the phone."

"Daddy! I knew you'd answer for me!"

"It's because I'm unavailable. Ha! Gotcha, didn't I? Leave me a message. I don't know how to check it, though. Matter of fact, just shoot me a text. I'm not going to check this. Peace!"

I stared at my phone's screen. I felt betrayed by it. Why didn't it work in a way that made my dad answer the phone?! I threw it across the room.

"Bae?" Charles called out to me. "I think you should take the day off. You're not going to work, are you?"

"Yeah. I am. I'm not going to stress about this. He's just laid up with a hoe like CJ said. Nothing can happen to him. Everywhere he goes, people know him. People are looking out for him everywhere. I'm going to go to work and get my mind off of this."

I showered, ate breakfast, brushed my teeth, and headed out the door. Charles met me at my car.

"Before you drive off, I want to pray for you."

"Okay."

I had been praying myself, but I couldn't pray hard enough or strong enough or long enough. I prayed every second of the day. God had to come through. He just had to.

"Lord, we thank you for another day. It's another day to get it right and be more like You. Lord, you know." Charles sighed. "You know all about it, Father. You know the pain my wife is experiencing. You know the things that she hasn't told anyone. I pray that You cover her in perfect peace. Wrap Your loving arms around her and soothe her soul. Please allow Your comfort to penetrate her mind and put her at ease. Anoint her with whatever she needs for her shift emotionally, spiritually, cognitively.

"And, Lord God, please give us answers. Please reveal to us where my father-in-law is. Cover him in your protection, God. Allow him a way out if he's found himself somewhere he can't get out of. Restore him unto himself and to us. Give us answers. Let him know that he can call us. That we aren't so mad at him that he can't come home. Please ease the hearts and minds of everyone affected. In Jesus' name. Amen."

"Amen. Thanks, Bae. I'll see you tonight."

The prayer worked. I was so at ease and at peace that I didn't even tell my boss, Lara, what was going on. My boss was one of my closest friends next to Que. She knew almost everything about me and what was going on. I didn't even think to tell her because I was at peace.

But all that changed once I got home. Charles met me at the door.

"No one has heard from him still, Ivory. Mama Jackie called me earlier and told me that she filed a missing persons report on him yesterday. It was officially twenty-four hours when she did it. It's time to tell Mychaela what's going on. Our daughter needs to know what's happening with Papa Curtis."

"Missing persons report?" I whispered.

It never dawned on me that my father was *missing*. Like… missing. Children who have their pictures on the wall at Walmart *missing*. People on the back of milk cartons *missing*. Amber alerts and silver alerts going off on your phone *missing*. Like search party *missing*. Like Lifetime movies *missing*.

This is the conversation that we were having. My father was… *missing.*

"Yes. And I don't know if you saw the newspaper today, but him being missing is the headline of today's paper."

I was still just stuck in shock when Charles placed the newspaper in my hand. It was front page news: **MADISON HEIGHTS, Mich. – Madison Heights police are asking for the public's help locating a 70-year-old man who went missing after an appointment in Detroit. Police are looking for Curtis Jones who hasn't been seen by his family since around 10 a.m. on Thursday, Feb. 13. We're told Curtis left his home that morning for an appointment at a hospital in Detroit. His wife saw him leave and says he appeared normal. Curtis left with his cell phone, but the phone has been off since he's been reported missing. Curtis checked into the hospital at 1 p.m. for his 1:20 appointment. Police say he checked out at 1:41. Curtis did not return home, and his family filed a missing person's report overnight. Curtis was last seen wearing a black winter hat, a black coat, blue sweater, blue pants, and blue dress shoes. He's 5 feet 9 inches tall and weighs 174 lbs. He left home driving a blue Ford pickup truck, double doors on the passenger side, with a Michigan handicap license plate. Below is a stock photo of the blue Ford pickup truck Curtis was last seen driving. The truck has a dent on the driver's side front bumper, and the double doors on the passenger side are also dented. Curtis is in good* *mental condition but has partial paralysis on his right side from a previous stroke. If you think you've seen Curtis or know of his whereabouts, call Madison Heights Police Department.*

His license plate number was printed in the paper, and a picture of him in the paper was staring me in my face. It was all surreal to me. I know I saw it with my eyes, but I still couldn't understand. How was this my life? How was this happening?

CJ lived in Detroit, and my dad's rental properties were in Detroit; therefore, he and CJ saw each other a lot. I lived in Canton, about a little over an hour away from Madison Heights where my dad lived. Because Daddy and CJ were in the same city frequently and went to church together, he saw him more, knew more about him than I did, and hung with him more. They often had breakfast and lunch together. I won't say that he knew him better than I did, but he definitely knew more and knew him pretty well.

I had avoided talking to his wife Jackie the day before. I don't really know why. We were close, so there was no beef or drama there. I guess I didn't want to hear her say what I'd been trying to deny. I'm assuming that's why I hadn't heard from her, either. Because she didn't want to tell me what she knew I didn't want to hear.

I called CJ instead of calling Jackie, even though I knew Jackie would have given me better answers.

"CJ," I said to my brother once he answered the phone. "What— I mean anything— I mean why— I mean—." I couldn't get my thoughts or words together. Truth be told, I don't know why I called him. I had a million questions and no questions at the same time.

"Ivory, slow down. My God. You are so damn dramatic."

"I'm not trying to be dramatic, CJ. I'm just worried about Daddy."

"Daddy is fine. How many times I have to tell you that?"

"You don't know that."

"I do know that, Ivory. Who is brave and bold enough to do something to Daddy? Not a soul. Everybody knows he doesn't leave the house without his gun. Everybody knows he ain't afraid to pull the trigger. He's just laid up with some whore. And now that Jackie has filed a missing person's report and got his face all over the city's newspaper and news, he surely isn't coming home now. He'll tuck his tail between his legs and come home in a few days."

"Curtis, Jr., I'm not saying that someone did anything to him. What if he had a heart attack? Another stroke? An aneurysm?"

"Ivory, if he had any of those things, that means that he would have been found by now. He would have been found in his car or in a bathroom or on aisle nine at Target. He didn't have a heart attack, stroke, or aneurysm. He had a good nut. Period."

"Wait. You said his face is all over the news?"

"Duh, Ivory. That is what happens when you are reported as missing. The news interviews the person closest to them, and they air it. What is wrong with you?!"

I had had enough of his snotty, flat, stank, nonchalant attitude drenched voice and demeanor. These things were not common sense to me. This was not my everyday life. This was the first time ever in my life that anyone had to be reported as missing. The most anyone had been missing was when my daughter Mychaela pulled away from me and ran around the side of the house. It took me five seconds to find her. Those five seconds felt like five years. But Daddy wasn't around the side of my house. He was missing.

"Bye, Curtis, Jr. Thank you for answering the phone."

I hung up before he could say anything in response.

My chest began to cave in. Him being reported missing and being on the news was making it more real than I was ready to accept. I had been avoiding it, but I knew that it was time to call Jackie.

"Hey, Ivory," Jackie answered the phone. "This is crazy, isn't it?" Her voice was slow and solemn.

Jackie was usually the life of the party. She was not the Debbie Downer or Negative Nancy. She was always upbeat and positive and had an encouraging word for you. This was not the Jackie I was used to. Hearing the melancholy in her voice made this all the more real.

I guess I expected her to answer all bubbly, telling me that this was all made up, a dream, a nightmare, a book… Something. But her voice… her voice said it all.

"You've heard *nothing*?" I asked her.

"Nothing," she replied.

"I'm sorry I haven't contacted you earlier. I guess I thought this would go away in a few hours."

"We all did, Ivory. That's why I hadn't contacted you. And I know I should have called you once I filed the missing person's report. My head hasn't been in the game. The only reason CJ knows is because Curtis' sister Amber called CJ to get the phone number to Curtis' reporter-friend who works at the news station. It took CJ forever to give Amber the number.

"CJ begged me not to report him as missing. He said people would start looking for him if I did that. I said, 'That's the point.' He said we shouldn't draw too much attention to it. But the longer we wait, the longer it'll take for him to show up, possibly. I don't know, Ivory. I just don't know what to do."

"You did the right thing, Jackie. And if something is wrong with him, or if he's… you know, and you didn't file the missing person's report, you would look suspicious. You did the right thing."

"Yeah. We've been driving around, looking for him. Some church members. Some family members. A few neighbors. Did you see the report on the news?"

"No. CJ just told me that it aired today. I didn't know."

"I figured you haven't. It aired on the six o'clock news, and I know you don't get off until about five thirty or so. It'll air again on the ten o'clock news. Amber did the interview with me. Curtis has good connections down there at the news station. They promised me that they would air it every day until he is found. They're probably going to air the same clip over and over. That's fine. I just want him to be found."

"Everyone knows and loves them some Curtis. Daddy makes a mark everywhere he goes."

"How can his loud mouth not?" Jackie laughed.

Jackie laughing somehow gave me permission to laugh.

"These are the facts." I laughed.

"Go get some rest or cook or do nothing, Ivory. Let the police do their job, okay?"

"Yes. Okay. I will come by and see you tomorrow if Daddy is still missing."

"Then I pray I don't see you tomorrow."

"I don't want to see you tomorrow, either."

"And if Curtis is here tomorrow, we will come by and eat up all your and Charles' food."

"I'm glad I just went grocery shopping."

There was awkward silence on the phone. I'm not sure how we got off the phone, but we did.

****

Daddy did his share of dirt in the streets, but he always came home to his wife Jackie. He especially wouldn't have missed Valentine's Day with her. Like clockwork, he was usually home by seven p.m. and asleep in his favorite recliner by the time the ten o'clock news aired. So, it was so eerie that this day, I was watching him on the ten o'clock news.

***Madison Heights Man Goes Missing, Leaving Family Desperate for Answers** was the headline of the ten o'clock news.

The news reporter announced, "A missing Madison Heights man's family is in agony this Valentine's Day. Loved ones of Curtis Jones are in shock, saying he is known for making everyone smile. But now they're driving around looking for him while police also investigate.

"Police say on Thursday afternoon, Jones checked into a hospital in Detroit for an appointment. He checked out about forty minutes later. His wife Jackie says several family members called him, but his phone went straight to voicemail, and they haven't heard from him since," the news reported.

The interview showed Jackie. "I really don't know what to feel. I'm in disbelief."

"That was his wife Jackie, who has spent the last twenty-five Valentine's Days with her husband Curtis.

The news showed Jackie again. "He is a nice, fun person. He's a grandfather and a dad."

The reporter stated, "But this time on Valentine's Day, she is surrounded by family and friends while her best friend is nowhere to be found."

Jackie stated, "This house is full of people, and we are just waiting on him. We just want him to come home."

My Aunt Amber, his sister, stated, "He's been a tremendous strength. He will make you smile when you're down, and that's needed."

The reporter stated, "Jones is a stroke survivor and is partially paralyzed on his right side. The family says Curtis overcame that adversity and does not struggle with any mental illnesses. Curtis' family is holding on to hope that their rock will come home fast."

His sister stated, "I tell you almost every day that I love you. Please know that and come back home. Please know that I need you, Jackie needs you."

The reporter reported, "The Jones family says he is about five feet, nine inches, and is wearing a black coat, a blue sweater, and blue pants.

They say he also likes to go sit by the water downtown."

The news really emphasized that he was missing in a blue Ford pickup truck. Pictures of his truck were plastered all over the news.

My God. This was real. This was happening. His phone wasn't going straight to voicemail at first. Now, it was. It either died or someone turned his phone off. Either way, he was really out of reach now.

Chapter 3

February 16, 2020
DAY 3- Sunday

After church, Charles, Que, and I drove around in separate cars looking for Daddy all around Detroit and surrounding areas. We searched the woods, abandoned buildings, alleys, everywhere. We weren't by ourselves. Communities and churches also joined us in our search.

He owned property near 7 Mile and Woodward. We all took turns searching that area particularly. It was as if everyone felt his spirit there. No matter how much we felt him, we never saw him.

Hours and hours of calling different people, searching different areas, and social media lurking all turned into dead ends. The police were a joke. They weren't doing shit. Random people were always calling into the station, saying they think they saw Daddy, but those were dead ends, too. This was the pattern every damn day. Look for him, and nothing. Stalk social media, and nothing. Call and harass people, and nothing. Call the police, and nothing. People "saw" him, and nothing.

Every damn day, it was *nothing.*

***Madison Heights Man Goes Missing, Leaving Family Desperate for Answers** was the headline of the six o'clock news.

The news reporter announced, "A missing Madison Heights man's family is in agony this Valentine's Day. Loved ones of Curtis Jones are in shock, saying he is known for making everyone smile. But now they're driving around looking for him while police also investigate.

"Police say on Thursday afternoon, Jones checked into a hospital in Detroit for an appointment. He checked out about forty minutes later. His wife Jackie says several family members called him, but his phone went straight to voicemail, and they haven't heard from him since," the news reported.

The interview showed Jackie. "I really don't know what to feel. I'm in disbelief."

"That was his wife Jackie, who has spent the last twenty-five Valentine's Days with her husband Curtis.

The news showed Jackie again. "He is a nice, fun person. He's a grandfather and a dad..."

And there his truck was *again*, plastered all over the news *again*.

I don't know why I tortured myself by watching that. Yes, I do. That day was Sunday, and I didn't work Sundays. I didn't have work to drown myself in. There were no coworkers to joke with and keep my mind off of things. I had to live in it. I had no choice but to absorb it. Maybe I was hoping that the news would say that he was found. But they didn't.

Daddy still was not home. No one had heard from him! His disappearance or missing— I'm not really sure what to call it—was all over the news and social media. We all were calling his phone, but it was going straight to voicemail. I called constantly, thinking he just was not answering the phone for them. *I'm his favorite. Maybe he'll answer for me.* I prayed and called repeatedly, hoping that one of those times he was gonna give in and answer just to put my fears to rest.

He didn't. His phone remained off.

I called CJ asking a barrage of the same questions that I'd been asking him for the last two days: When was the last time that you heard from him? Did he seem to be in his right mind? Where do you think he could have possibly gone? And every day, CJ would repeat, in his snotty voice, "Mmph! I'm telling you, he's just on a booty call gone wrong. He's probably with one of his women, and at this point, he sees he's let it go too far, so he's probably embarrassed."

I'm not sure if he knew something we didn't know, or if he was trying to convince himself that he was not missing, but his nonchalant attitude was asking for an ass whipping. Our dad was missing, and all he could think was he was knee-deep in some pussy. This was deeper than pussy. My gut was stirring up, and I knew that something was wrong. I wasn't sure what that *something* was, but it was definitely *something.*

"I don't trust that bitch," I told Que over the phone.

"I don't trust that bitch, either, Ivory. She ain't shit. Ain't never been shit and ain't gone be shit. Her mama ain't shit, either. But who we talking about, though?"

"Curtis, Jr.," I answered.

"Oh, I'm so sorry! I didn't know that we were talking about your brother. I didn't mean to call your mama a bitch. I'm sorry, Ms. Mama Luna."

"You didn't lie," I said.

"I know I didn't. I just would never say it out loud. To you. With knowledge of you hearing it. But I definitely would say it to others. No doubt."

"Well, that's sweet of you."

"Just call me Splenda. But what did CJ do now?"

"He's just too nonchalant and carefree about Daddy being missing. He brushes me off whenever I bring him up. He acts like I'm tripping or making this stuff up. It's all over the news at this point. Daddy is not here! You notice how everyone showed up to search for Daddy except CJ? He has *never* joined any of the searches."

"What do you think he has to do with it?"

"Hell, I don't know, Quantavia. Something."

"CJ is a lot of things, but a murderer isn't one. Liar? Yes. Manipulator? Of course. As crafty as the devil? You bet! But murder? No. Even he is not that evil."

"But what about torturing? Holding him hostage?"

"He's dumb as rocks. Torture and holding someone hostage is a mastermind's game. He can barely spell his own name."

I giggled. "You're right. I just want my daddy to come home. I'm thinking of all kinds of crazy stuff and pointing fingers at everybody I can't stand."

"That's understandable. But remember that his dad is missing, too. Everyone doesn't cope the same. CJ lies to everyone. Pretty sure he lies to himself, too."

"Ugh! I don't mind *you* being right. I just hate that you're right about him not being that evil."

"If I come to CJ's rescue, it's serious. You thought about going to therapy or counseling? This is a lot to bear, Ivy."

Only, and I mean only, Que could call me Ivy.

"Nah. It's not serious enough for that. I'll just keep talking to you and Charles."

"Should I make the invoice out to you, or you just gonna Cash App me?"

"I will pay you in Weight Watchers friendly home cooked meals."

"Sold! I'll accept. Food is a form of currency, and it's a language that I'm fluent in."

We got off the phone so Que could get ready for work. I appreciated everything about Que, but she was wrong. CJ was an evil witch who knew no boundaries in order to get what he wanted.

I remember when I first brought my husband home to meet my family, I could tell CJ was impressed. Charles drove a nice car, had a good paying job at a car company, came from a loving, close-knit family, dressed nice, smelled good, and was a man of God. He was marriage material.

Always looking for my brother's approval, I wanted him to like my boyfriend, but not in the way I perceived him to like him. Whenever in his presence, CJ looked at him a little too googly-eyed, laughed a little too hard at his jokes, and felt too damn comfortable inviting him to church events without me knowing. CJ was gay, loud, and proud. He never was in a closet, and he didn't hide himself for no one.

My suspicions of CJ wanting Charles for himself were debunked one night when we went to dinner in Mexican Village. I thought I sensed CJ kind of flirting with Charles, but I quickly discovered what was going on. Do you know this asshole had the audacity to invite him to a church function in front of me?! In front of me, CJ told Charles, "I've been watching you ever since you been coming around. You would get along so well with my choir member NaKia. She likes tall, dark, handsome men like you. Y'all would really gel.

Come to our Revival Monday at seven. You won't regret it. She'll be happy to meet you."

Well, on this particular night, I had one too many Long Island iced teas, so when CJ invited Charles to his church to meet a woman, I had some liquid courage to confront him. Man, I went the fuck off! Charles was trying to respectfully decline CJ's invitation, but I couldn't keep my mouth shut.

"How in the hell do you think it's okay to invite him and not invite me? How the fuck you gonna introduce him to another woman? And you're doing this in front of me! Bitch, I can hear yo' trashy ass! He's *my* boyfriend. He doesn't want to go anywhere with you without me going. He is not interested in other women."

His response was, "You don't even go to church. NaKia and Charles have more in common than the two of you."

I was too outdone with this bitch! I wanted to reach over the table and slap the shit out of him, but instead, Charles and I got up and left the restaurant, leaving his foul ass there by himself!

My mother, father, friends, and even Charles' parents had told me CJ was envious of me, but I could never understand why! My thinking was, *He's my brother. He isn't supposed to be envious of me. He's supposed to be my best friend, my ride or die, my supporter, my cheerleader. We're supposed to win together!* But when he pulled that shit trying to hook Charles up with NaKia, what everyone had been telling me for so many years suddenly became clear. He was jealous of me and wanted to be me and wanted whatever it was that I had.

CJ and I are six years apart. Growing up, we were all we had, so I could never understand why he hated me so much. As far as I can remember, he's treated me like shit! Like he despised my very existence.

Nothing I did was good enough. I always felt like I was trying to please him, looking for his acceptance, him to tell me I was pretty, or he was proud of me. But those things never came.

Growing up, I was high yellow, overweight, with a pudgy nose. My brother on the other hand was brown skinned, string bean skinny, with a long, flat nose. We didn't favor at all. As soon as my mother was out of sight, he would torture me by calling me Dirty Red, Fat, and Miss Piggy until I was in tears.

He is the same evil bitch now that he was then. But I'm not the same sensitive girl that I was back then. He's not sending me to bed crying anymore. I'm going to find out if and what he did to Daddy, I said to myself that day. And I meant it. Until I went to bed and realized that Que was right. Even this was beyond Curtis, Jr.

Chapter 4

February 17, 2020
DAY 4- Monday

***Madison Heights Man Goes Missing, Leaving Family Desperate for Answers** was the headline of the twelve o'clock news.

The news reporter announced, "A missing Madison Heights man's family is in agony this Valentine's Day. Loved ones of Curtis Jones are in shock, saying he is known for making everyone smile. But now they're driving around looking for him while police also investigate.

"Police say on Thursday afternoon, Jones checked into a hospital in Detroit for an appointment. He checked out about forty minutes later. His wife Jackie says several family members called him, but his phone went straight to voicemail, and they haven't heard from him since," the news reported.

The interview showed Jackie. "I really don't know what to feel. I'm in disbelief…"

I kept my father being missing a secret from my coworkers. I needed to have at least one safe space. The only person I eventually told was my boss Lara because she was one of my closest friends. She constantly offered me time off, but I always declined because I knew that all I would do was sit at home and cry. My boss had to tell my two supervisors about him being missing just in case I needed days off, they wouldn't trip. But that is all who knew. All three of them kept it hush-hush as I requested.

I lived in Canton, and my father and Jackie lived in Madison Heights, which is about an hour and a half for me to get to them. Starting from Day Three, I had been driving back and forth to sit with Jackie and help brainstorm on where he could possibly be.

There had always been chitter chatter about Daddy and Jackie possibly divorcing, so there just may have been some truth to what CJ had been saying about how he had moved on with another woman. There was even some talk about him having gone to see his brother in Arizona. Now if that was the case, where was the truck? He surely wouldn't drive that far. He would definitely fly.

We checked the airports and even called his brother Mason in Arizona. Uncle Mason was pissed because he said we were involving him in Daddy's mess, but who cares? We were trying to locate Daddy's whereabouts.

There was speculation that maybe Daddy could've taken an international trip, but then we realized that he didn't have his medicines. About twenty-five years prior to him going missing, he had a severe stroke, so he took a lot of medicines daily that he couldn't go without.

Realizing that he didn't have his medicines lead us to call his doctors and pharmacies to see when was the last time he'd gotten a refill. Nothing had been refilled, so that was a dead end. Looking through his medicines lead us to an unfamiliar pill bottle with the name Sandra Barker. *Who? What? Who in the hell is Sandra Barker?* Now we were doing some serious digging.

We looked up Sandra Barker on Facebook, and lo and behold, her profile picture was of my father standing in the door of an apartment. That came as a shock to all of us! We did some more digging by messaging her. We found out that Ms. Sandra Barker knew all of our names, our kids, and our husbands' names. Sandra said that she refused to speak to anyone of us other than CJ. WHAT THE FUCK?! Now we were really giving CJ the side-eye. Why was he the chosen one?

Whatever they talked about on the phone, no one will ever know. CJ snuck off on the phone with Sandra for nearly two hours. When he returned, all he said was, "Sandra doesn't know where Daddy is." And that was that. We never heard from Sandra again.

Chapter 5

February 18, 2020
DAY 5- Tuesday

Knock, knock, knock.

I woke up from my sleep, looked at the clock that read 4:04 a.m., looked at Charles sleeping, and decided that I was tripping. Charles could hear roaches blinking in his sleep, so if he didn't hear knocking at the door, I was tripping.

Knock, knock, knock. There it was again! I opened the doorbell camera app on my phone to see who was at the door.

"Daddy!" I jumped out of my skin, bed, the air, left a few extensions behind, and raced to the door.

"Hey, Bay-beeee!" he greeted me as he always had.

My mind was everywhere. I couldn't process it. I was in awe, shock, disbelief—everything. I was trying to form words, but nothing came out. I just stared at him with my mouth open.

"A mosquito is going to fly in your mouth if you don't shut it."

I leaped towards him, kissed him on the lips, and said in his ear, "You know me and Charles do nasty stuff with my mouth."

"Ugh! Yuck!" He laughed, wiped my kiss off, and spit.

This was our regular greeting. My dad was back. My God, my dad was back!

"I know I got some explaining to do." He looked down at his shoes. "I don't even know where to start."

My daddy was the biggest liar I ever knew. Not only was he the biggest liar, he was the best liar. He could look you straight in the face, cry, tremble, throw shit, run his blood pressure up, have a mini-stroke, and still be lying. So, whatever he said, no matter how good he sold it, I couldn't believe it. I knew that I had to just be satisfied with him being back.

"Come on in, Daddy."

"You sure? I don't want to wake Franky or My Main Man up."

He called my daughter Franky—short for Frankenstein—because he said she had a big square head. It sounds cruel, but it was really cute, and my daughter loved it. He called Charles My Main Man because they were damn near best friends.

"They wouldn't mind being woken up for this. Are you crazy?! Get in here!"

He plopped down on the couch and put his feet up on the ottoman. He laid his head back and sighed.

"Start talking, Old Man!" I squealed.

I jumped up and sat on his lap. I was so excited I couldn't contain myself. I was jittery, antsy, angry, confused, excited, mad, sad, nauseous… Whew.

"Get off me, Old Woman!" He teased and playfully threw me to the floor.

"Let's take a selfie!" I couldn't stop squealing.

Selfies were our thing. We had to selfie everywhere. While cooking, driving, eating, walking, on FaceTime, arguing— everything and everywhere. We were getting back to our old selves, to our usual routines.

He gladly pulled out his phone and made a funny face beside mine. We took about sixteen selfies in one sitting. We went through them, and he told me he would send them to me to post them on social media later. He said he wanted that to be the announcement that he was back, alive, and well.

"Start talking, Old Man!"

"I mean, you keep cutting off my opportunity to say something, Ivory. Shit! Shut up!"

"I know. I'm sorry. I just… I thought I'd never see you again. And here you are. I can't stop looking at you and touching you."

"That's what she said."

"Ugh! Stop being a whore for three seconds, please, Daddy."

"I can't do nothing in three seconds." He laughed his hearty laugh.

"Focus, Curtis! Seriously, are you okay?"

"Don't I look okay? What would happen to me?"

"I don't know. Where the hell you been?"

"Ivory. Who you talking to?" Charles asked, groggily, sleep still lingering in his eyes and throat.

"There he go! I missed you, My Main Man! Let me show you these women who did something strange for a li'l bit of change." Daddy took out his phone and went to some pictures. "Look at this. I would have emptied out all my savings if they asked me to."

Charles didn't move. He was in shock. But that was Daddy. He always kept life moving like nothing happened.

But that was Daddy's and Charles' usual greeting. Daddy would show Charles some nudes on the phone, they'd tell filthy jokes to each other, then Daddy would tell me I had myself a good man.

Daddy was trying to get back in the swing of things, but Charles couldn't. He needed answers. Charles possibly cried over Daddy's missing more than me. He thought about it and was affected by it just as much as me. So, no, Charles couldn't just "fall back in line". He needed to know what happened, starting with Day One.

"Charles," I said, "go look at the women on the phone. You know Daddy always gotta show you."

Charles still didn't move. He just stared at me. He was a statue. His face showed no emotion. His body showed no expression.

"Charles!" I screamed.

"Who are you talking to in here, Ivory?"

I scoffed. "You're going to act like you don't see Daddy sitting right here? I know he has some explaining to do, but come on. At least acknowledge him."

"Let's go back to bed, Ivory. I'll fix you some skim milk."

"No! I'm talking to my daddy! What is wrong with you?"

"Baby, Curtis isn't here," he whispered to me.

"Yes, he is! He's right there!" I pointed to the couch… The *empty* couch. "Turn the light on, Charles!"

Charles turned the light on. I quickly looked at the couch… The *empty* couch.

"You scared him away! You came in here being ugly and ran him away! He came back!"

"Ivory, no one was here, Bae."

"Yes, he was! My daddy came back! He always comes back for me! See?!"

I pulled up the doorbell camera app to show him that Daddy had come. I rewound to a little before when I opened the door. Nothing was there. I rewound a little more. Nobody was there. I frantically kept rewinding the footage to show Charles. I scratched the phone screen trying to show him. Did Charles erase the footage?! Who tampered with the evidence?!

"He was here!"

"Babe, come on to bed. You're just tired. It's okay. You've been through a lot. Just come lay next to me."

"What's going on?" Mychaela asked, as she walked into the living room.

"Nothing. Go back to bed, Toots. You have to wake up in about an hour to get ready for school."

"Okay, Dad," Mychaela said, hesitatingly.

Charles walked me back to bed. When I looked at the clock, it read 4:20 a.m. How could those sixteen minutes feel like two hours? I thought I had my dad back for two hours. I had the happiest two hours, a.k.a. sixteen minutes, of my life that I hadn't had in a week. Why did Charles have to disturb me?

I tossed and turned for the next forty minutes or so. Charles just let me be. He knew that I was at the point of no comforting. There were no more magic words that could be said to me. He had to just let me be.

I had to get up and get moving for work at five a.m. It was a big day that day. The owners were flying in from Los Angeles, and I had to go in early to make sure the store looked better than perfect. I worked at a grocery store as a Community Outreach and Donations Coordinator. I had to show them why I was the best at doing what I do.

I always had to have some kind of noise to get going. Radio, TV, box fan, something. Since the remote was right beside the bed, I turned the TV on.

As soon as I did, the news reporter announced, "A missing Madison Heights man's family is in agony this Valentine's Day. Loved ones of Curtis Jones are in shock, saying he is known for making everyone smile. But now they're driving around looking for him while police also investigate…"

This just couldn't last too much longer. My daddy always came back for me. Always.

Chapter 6

February 19, 2020
DAY 6- Wednesday

Work was no longer the thing that kept me going. It no longer kept my mind occupied. The people I interacted with on the daily were no longer the highlight of my day. My coworkers had become like the annoying neighbors who won't shut up. I got tired of seeing so many damn customers coming in and out of the store. Why did the checkout line have to beep every time something was rung up? Why did the scanner have to make so much damn noise every time the barcode was scanned? Why were the lights so damn bright? Just… UGH!

I went into the attic of the store where miscellaneous things were kept. I went there to escape but still could pass it off as if I was working. I could say that I was looking for twist ties if I got caught. I knew that something as small as twist ties would take a while to find, so that was the perfect lie if asked why I was gone for so long. I needed a few seconds or minutes or hours to myself.

To be able to back up my lie of "looking for twist ties", I began looking through the mounds and piles of crap that were stored in the attic. With every little thing that I moved out of my way, I felt better and better. When I moved the crate over, I felt better. When I scooted the folding chair over, I felt better. When I lifted up pots and pans, I felt better.

Something clicked in my head that said, "Knock all this shit over and see how good you'll really feel." I did it. And I did it again. And I did it again.

I kicked shit over. I knocked shit over. I punched some unknown object. I slung some foreign object from one wall to the next. It felt good as fuck. Until the door came swinging open. It was my boss Lara. My closest friend at work. A true friend outside of work.

She looked at me, and I looked at her. My chest caved in, and I couldn't control my cry. If you can even call it a cry. It was a shrill. A yell. A roar. My knees gave out, and I laid on the floor, belly to wood.

Lara got on her knees beside me and placed her hand on my back. "Ivory," she said in her Haitian accent, "I don't know how to pray in English. I only know how to pray to Jesus in Haitian. Do you mind if I do that?"

"No, I don't mind," I whispered.

I needed all the Jesus I could get, especially because I slowly was forgetting how to get Him for myself.

I don't know what she prayed, but the atmosphere shifted. I was able to get off the floor and stand on my feet. I honestly don't remember if I thanked her or hugged her. I was in my own zone, on autopilot. If I didn't thank or hug her, I pray she knows how much that meant to me. I pray she knows what it did to me and for me. I pray she understood that I just wasn't myself; I wasn't trying to be rude. I just wanted my daddy back.

It had been almost a week, and according to the detective who received no new leads, the number of leads tend to decrease after the first seventy-two hours of an investigation. But with the help of our church families, friends, and social media, the search was still going strong. Everyone was prayerful and hopeful that he'd turn up. At this point, everybody was looking for the blue Ford pickup truck. We were continuing to receive leads daily, but unfortunately, none of them led to bringing my father back home.

This daily holding pattern had everyone's nerves on edge. It was like watching a horror movie on repeat without knowing the outcome. We needed to turn the search up a notch, but CJ was holding on to "he's with one of his girlfriends", which contributed to some of the families' relaxed sense of urgency.

When I got to my father's house that day, the news station was there to help further the search and keep the story relevant. Jackie and two of my father's sisters were on the news pleading with the world that if they knew something or had seen anything, to please speak up. "We just want to bring him home. We don't want to press charges. We aren't even seeking justice at this point. Just return him to us."

All of my siblings were there but CJ. CJ said he wasn't going to be wasting a perfectly good evening searching for anyone who is somewhere at a cumfest. "I'm going to spend my day busting nuts just like him," he told Jackie, our two sisters, and me.

I don't even know how he could even think about sex, orgasms, intimacy, etcetera. Even if Daddy was laid up with somebody, we didn't know that for sure, so we had to move and react as if he was in imminent danger. I was married, and sex hadn't crossed my mind since that day he went missing. CJ didn't even have a steady boyfriend, and he was getting it in.

Maybe I was jealous of CJ and angry at myself. Jealous that his life was moving on while mine was in a whirlwind standstill. Angry at myself for not being as optimistic as him and allowing my life to be so drastically affected.

Maybe it was me. Maybe I was overreacting. Maybe I was doing too much and thinking too extreme. Maybe it didn't take all that.

But maybe it did.

Chapter 7

February 20, 2020
DAY 7- Thursday

Charles told me to try my best to find the joy in the smallest of things. To see the silver lining whenever and wherever I could. This particular day I chose to take his advice. The first joy was that it was Day Seven. In the Bible, the number seven represents completion. I had faith that it was the end, and it would end the way I wanted it to, the way that I wrote it.

The second joy I had that day was a Creole customer came in and gave me her chili recipe. I didn't know much about people from Louisiana, but one thing I did know was that they ate everything spicy. She promised me that the chili was the right amount of seasonings and spices that complemented the savory-ness. She gave me her word that it wasn't too spicy for me and that I would love it.

The third joy I had that day was my daughter placed number one in her swim competition. It was proof that whatever the devil was trying to do, he wasn't going to succeed.

The fourth joy I had that day was church members, neighbors, and other people told me that they continued their searches for Daddy like they had been doing, and they didn't find him. The great thing about that is that they didn't find him dead. It was a wonderful day.

Then I went home…

The news reporter announced, "A missing Madison Heights man's family is in agony this Valentine's Day. Loved ones of Curtis Jones are in shock, saying he is known for making everyone smile. But now they're driving around looking for him while police also investigate.

"Police say on Thursday afternoon, Jones checked into a hospital in Detroit for an appointment. He checked out about forty minutes later. His wife Jackie says several family members called him, but his phone went straight to voicemail, and they haven't heard from him since…," the news reported.

And the news went on and on.

I found no more joy that day. I couldn't even conjure up the strength to make that chili. Damn "joy". Damn a silver lining. Damn it all to hell!

My daddy was missing. No phone calls. No texts. No smoke signals. No telegrams. No pigeons with notes in their mouths. No messages in a bottle. No "sliding in my DMs".

Joy could kiss my ass.

I went to sit and talk with Jackie. On this particular day, I remember there were a group of Jackie's lifelong friends: Patricia, Victoria, Lady J, Renita, Lexi; and her sisters Katrina, Clarissa, and Sherri in the kitchen running down every possible scenario that we could think of. We had called the airports, checked his credit cards, and none of his clothes or suitcases were missing, so he couldn't have taken a trip as CJ was now throwing out there. And most importantly, Daddy didn't have his many needed daily medications. Even if Daddy was taking a trip without any clothes, he would not have left his meds. So, we were back at square one.

"Maybe he is at one of his girlfriend's houses. Maybe he has clothes there already, and he's finally gone through with the threat of leaving Jackie. Maybe at his appointment, he told the doctor that he lost all of his meds, and his doctor wrote him new prescriptions," Clarissa suggested.

Jackie said, "Well, shit! He didn't have to do all of this. I would've taken him to the airport to be with the hussy, and I would have picked him up when he was done with her. I would've been okay with him going to stay somewhere. He didn't have to do all this! This isn't like Curtis, though. Even when he does dirt, he always comes home. Something is wrong." She began to cry, "I just want my husband to come home."

I asked Jackie, "If he walks through that door right now and says, 'I know I fucked up', would you forgive him?"

With huge crocodile tears running down her face, she said, "Absolutely. We've been married for twenty-six years and together for thirty-six years. I take care of Curtis. I love my husband. I'm the one who takes care of him."

She was trying not to break down, and we didn't know what in the hell to say. Everything had been said that there was to say. There was nothing we could do but pray. At this time, we were hanging on to all hope that he was going to one day stroll through the door as if none of this ever happened.

"But something is wrong," Jackie said, breaking the silence. "I know it. He always calls. He always comes home. He always sends a text, even though he knows how much I hate texting. I have to accept it. We all have to accept it. Curtis is dead."

"No! He is not!" I interjected.

"Jackie, don't say that," Clarissa begged. "We still have to hang on to hope."

"Y'all can hang on to hope as long as you want. But he is dead," she whispered.

"He's not," I argued.

"He's dead to me, Ivory! He is dead to me! In my opinion, he is dead! That is the only explanation. He is no longer with us. I have to let him go. This week has been torture. We all would feel better if we just accept what is in front of our faces. He may not be dead to y'all, but he is definitely dead to me."

Her body went limp, and she fell over on me, bawling her eyes out to the point of them being red and purple. I was no help. I had nothing I could say to her. There was nothing I could say to myself. If my dad being dead to her was what would ease her mind and give her peace at night, so be it.

In spite of all that Daddy had done, Daddy loved Jackie. There was absolutely no question about that. It was understandable why she would think that because he would never purposely go missing. He would never put Jackie through that. Never.

Chapter 8

February 21, 2020
DAY 8- Friday

Nothing. Absolutely nothing. No thing. Not hing. Nada. None. Nunca. Just. Nothing. The only thing that I could rely on was the same ole same ole, "A missing Madison Heights man's family is in agony this Valentine's Day. Loved ones of Curtis Jones are in shock, saying he is known for making everyone smile. But now they're driving around looking for him while police also investigate…

It was Friday. Daddy loved to party every Friday night. He found every party there was in the city. If music and women were there, so was Daddy. This day, Charles and I drove separately to every club, lounge, and house party that we found out about to look for Daddy.

I missed Daddy so much that every older man looked like him. Whenever I would see a man in a fedora, I got excited, thinking it was him. Whenever I saw a man with a gray beard, I thought it was him. Whenever I saw an older man dancing with a young woman, I knew for sure it was Daddy.

But it was never Daddy.

At every club, lounge, and party, I would ask the DJ to announce on the mic that Curtis Jones was needed at the DJ's booth. He never came. A Curtis Johnson came. A Cornelius James came. A

John Curt came. A Kirk Johns came. But never a Curtis Jones. Never Daddy.

On my way out of one of the clubs, a twenty-something year old lady stopped me at the door. "Your stepmom came to see me yesterday."

"Who are you?"

"I'm sorry. I'm Byresha. I'm a psychic. You're looking for your dad. I told her that he is alive, but he is not well. He is being held hostage. I don't know where they're holding him hostage, but there is a group of people trying to make him do something he doesn't want to do. It's all behind some money and assets. They want him to sign it over. They want it to all be theirs whenever he dies."

Daddy owned a lot of houses and land. He had a lot of assets. And his affairs were always in legal order. He believed in having things documented and notarized. So, it made sense that someone would want him to change the paperwork and sign everything over to them for whenever he died. Who would want that isn't the question because *everyone* wants money, houses, land, and assets. I would be up all night trying to figure that out. The question was where was he. I could take it from there if I had that answer.

"But how are they keeping him hostage?"

"They're keeping him drugged. Before it wears off, they're injecting him with something else. He can't physically move. And he also has been without his medications. That isn't safe.

There's a chance that if he isn't found soon, just being without his meds will kill him."

I didn't know that Jackie went to a psychic. I'm not surprised that she didn't tell me. She was a devout Christian, and she was probably embarrassed that she went to one. We were all at our wit's end, doing things that were out of our character. I looked at Jackie no differently for going to a psychic. I was just upset that I hadn't thought about it first. But Jackie must not have believed her because Jackie was sure that he was dead despite this psychic saying he was still alive.

"How do you know who I am?" I asked her.

"I'm psychic." She laughed. "I just know. But don't tell her you ran into me. She wanted this to be a secret."

"I won't. Thank you for your time."

I called Charles once I left there. We agreed to meet up at a waffle joint. All of this detective work had us hungry. I told him what the psychic told me, and he only nodded his head.

"You don't think there's some truth to it?" I asked him.

"I just don't trust people who call themselves psychics. They prey on the sad, vulnerable, helpless, hopeless people."

"How did she know I was his daughter?"

"Jackie could have shown her a picture of you. Psychics always ask for pictures of the family to 'see things better'."

"You don't believe in psychics anyway."

"I don't believe in going to them. I do believe that some people do have that gift. That's in the Bible. But knowing who's real and who's fake is the great divide," Charles said.

"But what if she's real?"

"She's real, but can't tell you where he's at? She's real, but can't tell you who 'they' or 'them' are? Even if she is real, she ain't told us shit. She ain't told us how to go get him. She hasn't told us how to rescue him. She hasn't told us how to get him back in our motherfucking house! She hasn't told us how to reach him, call him, laugh with him, or shoot the shit with him!"

Charles was slamming his fist on the table. His tears hit the table each time before his fist did. Charles was not a crier at all. If he was crying, it was a deep, serious, agonizing pain that he couldn't swallow. When I saw those tears, I knew that he had been feeling emotions that he hadn't let me in on. Not because he was trying to "be strong" for me or because he didn't want to bother me. He wanted to be there for me, so he pushed his emotions aside. But tonight… tonight, he couldn't.

"It doesn't matter if she is right," Charles continued. "She still hasn't helped us one bit with that gray ass 'revelation'. Lead us to him, and then she'll have my attention!"

I sat back, saying nothing. What could I say? He was right. At the end of the day, she still had not helped us, and we still were right where we started from.

"There was this man at the club tonight. He looked just like him, Ivory. Just like him. I pulled him by his collar, dragged him out of the club past everybody, and threw him in my car." He paused to catch his breath and wipe his face. "The man kept yelling, 'I ain't who you think I am! I swear to God I ain't him!'

"I wasn't trying to hear him. I dragged him by his collar from the front of the club, through the parking lot, into my car. I screamed at this man, 'Call me My Main Man! Say it! Say it! Curtis, why the fuck you doing this to us?! You know who I am! I'm your main man. Say it! Say that I am your main man!' When I focused on this man, he looked to be twenty-seven years old, had green highlights in his hair, and had a mouth full of golds. He didn't look like Curtis at all. Not even in the worst way.

"I'm out here snatching up innocent people. I'm snapping on folks at work. I can't even hear God's voice anymore, and I'm a deacon. So, I don't want to hear about some psychic who knows everything but don't know shit!"

I understood that Curtis was my daddy, but Daddy was Charles' best friend. His confidant. His shopping partner. The person he talked shit with and joked inappropriately. Whenever anything good happened, oftentimes, Charles told Daddy before he told me. Me being Daddy's daughter, there were limitations to our relationship. Daddy and Charles being best friends and both men meant there were no limitations to their relationship. Everything was on the table between them. Nothing was a secret. I'm not downplaying my pain; I just realized at that moment that Charles' pain and my pain couldn't compare. It was apples and oranges.

Charles ate his waffles and eggs without saying anything else. I did the same.

Chapter 9

February 22, 2020
DAY 9- Saturday

"I'm dreaming, aren't I?" I asked Daddy.

"Yea, Bay-beeee, you are."

"I don't care. As long as I get to have you. Please don't tell me that you are only going to show up in my dreams. Please don't tell me that this is the only way I can see you."

He said nothing.

"I'll take it. It's better than nothing."

"I mean, me in any form is a blessing. I'm a blessing. I'm Curtis motherfucking Jones in this bitch. Shiiiiit. You're welcome."

I snickered at him just being him. Who I remembered. Who I missed. He was the cockiest, hoeing, most lying person I'd ever met. And I loved him more than I loved anyone else outside of my husband and daughter.

"I've been exercising," he said.

A lie.

"And lifting weights, too."

Another lie.

"And I've been eating meat with bones it," I lied back.

"I would pay to see that." He laughed that hearty laughed that I missed hearing for the last nine days.

"I'm sorry, Ivory."

"For what?"

"Oh, just everything. Not this. I had nothing to do with this. I'm sorry about the other stuff."

"What other stuff?"

We went back and forth about what he was sorry for, for a few minutes, but he never gave me an answer. He talked in circles. I don't know what he was apologizing for. I never found out.

"Where are you? What happened? Why did you disappear?" I asked him.

"Well, I went to my appointment at the hospital. Everything went fine. After the appointment, I met up with—"

"Noooooo!" I screamed, as the alarm went off, breaking my dream.

Charles didn't budge. He just turned over and held me. "We're going to find him, Ivory. I promise."

"I know. But in what condition? What status? Will he even know himself? Will we recognize him? It's been nine days, Charles. Nine days!"

"Whatever condition or state he comes back in will be less agonizing than us not knowing anything at all. In the meantime, I will go with you to therapy. And I'll go with you as frequently and as long as you want."

I know he meant well. And I had nothing against therapy. But what would I even say to the therapist? Where would I begin? What would we do?

"Remember how much therapy helped us when our son died, Ivory?"

"I do. I guess going to therapy will be admitting that my dad is... missing. Gone."

"We're beyond that point now, Bae. We are aware. It is obvious now that he is missing. We all are feeling it. I need therapy myself. I'm going to go. Come with me. Just to be by my side."

"Okay. Let me know when, and I'll be there."

I'm not doubting that Charles needed therapy. I just know that the only reason he was going to go was to get me there. I knew in my heart that I wasn't going to go to therapy, and he knew, too.

Twenty-one years earlier, my eleven-month-old son Javaughn died from respiratory failure. I literally lost my mind. I had gotten to the point that I didn't even know my name. One day, I looked at Charles and asked him who was he. My mind had left me. I checked in from time to time, but most of the time, I was delirious.

I went to therapy, and it helped me. Helped isn't the word. It restored me. It brought me back to me. My husband got his wife back. My parents got their daughter back.

So, I believe in therapy. Therapy works. I have nothing against therapy. I just didn't need it. Yes, I was becoming delirious like I had with

Javaughn's death. Yes, I was losing myself like I did with Javaughn's death. Yes, I was crying all the time and was so down that I had to look up to see the ground just like with Javaughn's death. But I didn't need therapy. I just needed answers. I needed my daddy, no matter the condition or status.

Chapter 10

February 23, 2020
DAY 10- Sunday

The news reporter announced, "A missing Madison Heights man's family is in agony this Valentine's Day. Loved ones of Curtis Jones, are in shock, saying he is known for making everyone smile. But now they're driving around looking for him while police also investigate.

"Police say on Thursday afternoon, Jones checked into a hospital in Detroit for an appointment…"

I was at my wit's end. I didn't care what CJ or anyone else said. Daddy was not alright. He would not do this. Pussy would not have him treating us like this. Damn the search parties. It was time to play dirty.

"Ms. Angie. It's Ivory," I said over the phone. "I need a favor. Name your price. I don't care."

"I'm listening."

"You still work at the hospital?" I asked her.

"Yes."

"Check the records and see who had appointments before and after Daddy that day. Check surveillance to see if he left with anybody. Check the doctor's records to see if Daddy was told any disturbing news that may have caused him to take his own life. Get me whatever you can. I don't care how small. Get me information."

"Okay. I don't work in any of those departments, so give me until the end of the day to get all this to you."

"Thank you."

"You have Cash App?" Ms. Angie asked me.

"Yes, I do."

She gave me her information and told me that it'd be seven hundred dollars because I was putting her job at risk. I was prepared to pay her two thousand dollars, so I gladly sent her that seven hundred.

About thirty minutes later she called me with information about three men and one woman who had appointments around the same time as him. If they had appointments at around the same time, they were waiting in the lobby at the same time. Ms. Angie gave me their names, phone numbers, email addresses, and residential addresses. I wasn't going to be stupid enough to send them an email because that was traceable back to me which could trace back to her and get her fired. But I surely didn't mind calling them.

Ms. Angie called every one of them on three-way so that hospital's number would show up on their caller IDs, and she muted her phone.

I put on my best professional White Suzy voice and got to work. "Mr. Bingham?"

"Yes, this is he."

"Hi. This is Rebecca calling from the downtown hospital. How is your day going?"

"Oh, I can't complain."

"That's great to hear. I'm sorry to bother you. I don't know if you're aware about Curtis Jones being missing or if you even know who that is."

"Aw, Sweetheart. Who the hell don't know Curtis Jones? He ain't the tallest man, but his presence makes up for it. I've watched them talk about him on the news three times a day for about the last week now. I was just talking to him that day while we waited on the doctor."

"Well, we're trying to help the family find him. Did he tell you where he was going after the appointment? Did he seem like he wanted to take his own life?"

"Oh, no, Ma'am. He was full of life. I know they say you never know who is suicidal, but take my word for it: he was not suicidal. He didn't say where he was going per se. Just saying he was ready to grab something to eat and see his grandbabies. General conversation."

"Can you think harder?" I asked him, voice cracking, tears threatening to fall.

Mr. Bingham was quiet for about thirty seconds, then said, "No, Ma'am. I'm sorry. We didn't talk about anything particular. Just general conversation."

"No rush, Mr. Bingham. Take your time. Think."

"Miss, I told you what I know. If I think of anything, you have my word that I'll call the news station myself. He's a good man, and I want him home, too."

I sighed. "Thank you. Have a great day."

"You ready for me to call the next one, or you need a minute?" Ms. Angie asked me.

"Go to the next one, please."

"Okay."

Ms. Angie dialed a number on three-way and muted herself.

"Hello?"

"Ms. Andrade?"

"Yes?"

"Hi. I am Rebecca from the downtown hospital. How is your day?"

"It was good until you called me. I'm waiting on some results. You calling me with good news or bad news?

"Neither. I'm sorry to bother you. I don't know if you're aware that our patient Curtis Jones is missing, or if you even know who that is."

Ms. Andrade exhaled a sigh heavy with sorrow. "Yes, I know who he is. And I saw it on the news a few times. I'm aware that he is missing."

"I know that you two had an appointment around the same time, so I assumed that you maybe said a few words to each other in the lobby while you waited."

"We said more than a few words. We made plans to go fishing next weekend. My husband will be in town from work, and we were going to join Curtis and his wife Jackie on the boat that he said they just bought. We also—." She broke down crying.

I placed my phone on mute so that she wouldn't hear me crying. I cried so much those days that I lost track as to why I was crying. I think I was crying that time because it meant so much to me to know that someone other than family cared so much about my daddy.

She continued, "We also showed each other pictures of our grandbabies. We talked about how we like them so much more than we like our own kids." Ms. Andrade forced out a laugh. "We also talked about that new restaurant that opened downtown, and he said he was going once he left. Well, it was new to us. Could've been there for years for all we know."

"What restaurant, Ms. Andrade?"

"Junkie is the name of the restaurant."

"Did he say he was meeting anyone there?"

"No. I'm not even sure he had real plans on going. I said something about how fancy it looked, and he said he would go once he left his appointment to check it out."

"Did he seem suicidal?"

"Ha! Curtis? He was too cocky to kill himself that's for damn sure. Curtis was convinced the world would stop without him."

Boy was she right about that.

"No, he didn't seem suicidal at all. Someone has done something to him. He's not a person that you would expect to go missing. It has to be someone he knows and trusts. Because not just anybody could harm him. Everyone knows he never left the house without a gun. He let his guard down with somebody. That's the only thing that would make sense."

My chest sunk in. It never occurred to me that someone he knew, loved, and trusted would be capable of harming him. But that made sense. Daddy wasn't a guy who could be overtaken in the streets because, like Ms. Andrade said, he always carried a gun and wouldn't hesitate to pull the trigger if he thought he was in danger. Like she said, he let his guard down because he knew that person. But who and why?

"Ms. Andrade, we are so appreciative of your time. If you think of anything that could help us find him and bring this family rest and justice, please inform the police."

"Honey, you bet I will. As a matter of fact, I called that restaurant myself. Junkie restaurant. And asked them to review surveillance. They said they never saw him on camera, and they have no credit or debit card transactions with his name. I've been doing my part."

"Thank you so much and prayers on the results that you're waiting on."

"Thank you, Sweetie. Bye bye."

"Maybe you should take a break, Ivory," Ms. Angie suggested.

"No! Call the next one."

Ms. Angie called the next person, and he was of zero help. He didn't know who we were talking about and said that he slept in the lobby while waiting on the doctor. He said he talked to no one.

The next man answered the phone, saying, "I don't want to extend my car warranty. Bye."

He thought I was a telemarketer. I called him back. He answered the phone yelling again. He did it the third time as well. I said, *Fuck it. I'm pulling up at his house.* Ms. Angie begged me not to go. Said the guy sounded angry and she was afraid of what he'd do to me. She pleaded with me to wait for Charles to get home so that he could go with me. I told her that the way I felt, not even a gang could take me down.

I was so out of it mentally that I don't even remember driving to the man's house. I just showed up there somehow, and we began talking.

"Hi. I'm Ivory Stevans. I'm looking for Joey Summers. I am the daughter of Curtis Jones."

The man's body thumped against the doorframe, and he covered his mouth, eyes expanded.

"Was he found?" he whispered.

"No. You knew him?"

"Whew. Thank God. There's still a chance that he's alive." He leaned his head against the doorframe to gain his composure. "Yes, I knew him. We talked in the lobby the day that he went missing. Would you like to come in, Ivory?"

Joey looked to be about thirty-three years young. Tall, athletic, muscular build. He had youth and strength on his side. No way I could fight him off of me if he tried something. I was grieving, but I wasn't stupid. Even though I *felt* like a gang couldn't take me down because I was so amped up, I had enough sense to know that a gang could. I had enough sense to know that one man could. I stayed my ass outside on Joey Summer's porch.

"No, thank you. I don't want to come in. Just wanting to know if you had anything that could help us find him."

"No, I'm sorry. We walked to our cars from the appointment. He said he was meeting his son Curtis, Jr. for lunch at Bangy's restaurant. That's all I got. I am so sorry."

My ears exploded. My sight was a kaleidoscope. Nothing was functioning in my body. I couldn't hear, see, smell, think—nothing.

"Ivory. You okay?"

"Curtis, Jr. said nothing about them meeting up." I gulped.

"No disrespect, Ivory. But you know your daddy. He probably made a detour. You know how he was about them young women. That meet-up with your brother probably never happened."

I forced a smile. "You're right. Thank you for your time." I waved him off and sped to Bangy's.

Even if they never met up, CJ never mentioned that they were supposed to meet up and that he never showed up. I was on a mental flight when I walked into Bangy's, demanding to see surveillance footage from that day. I don't recall who I talked to or who said what. But I do recall seeing Daddy and CJ on tape at Bangy's, arguing about something. There was no audio on the video, but it was clear that CJ and Daddy were there, at that restaurant, after his appointment. CJ looked like he was about to blow a gasket from anger, and Daddy looked like he was shocked and appalled at what was coming out of CJ's mouth. They left together, got in their own cars, and from the few feet of surveillance that the restaurant's camera obtained, CJ followed Daddy in his car in a rage.

I immediately called Jackie.

"Jackie! Tell CJ to get to your house, now!"

"Ohhhkayyy. Why are you yelling at me?"

I took a second to exhale and gather myself. "I'm sorry. I'm so sorry, Jackie. It's nothing towards you at all."

"Why is he coming to my house?"

"We have something to tell you."

"Why can't you call him and tell him to come to my house?"

"Because he won't. You know how he is about me. He won't do anything I ask of him."

"Okay," she said, hesitatingly.

I wasn't trying to put Jackie in our mess, but we needed answers. We needed peace. We needed to know where the fuck my daddy was!

"And I'm sorry for exploding the other day, Ivory. I don't believe he is dead. He is not dead to me. He is very much alive. I'm still holding on to hope. I'm still praying and believing God for a miracle. I believe in my heart of hearts that he is alive. I just had a moment. You are going through your own turmoil, and I lost it. I'm sorry for putting all that on you."

"Jackie, we all have had our breaking points. I know you will never let him go. He is your world. He has to be. All that you've put up with. It is fine. I forgive you, but there is nothing to apologize about. I am on my way to you. See you in a bit."

On the way to Jackie's house, Ms. Angie called me. She apologized to me, saying that the hospital's cameras showed nothing. He came in and left peacefully. There was nothing that would draw suspicions. Ms. Angie also checked the notes from that appointment, and nothing bad was documented. It was a regular check-up, and everything was fine. No new meds were prescribed. The doctor didn't write any prescriptions at all. So, he didn't receive any news that would make him want to harm himself, and he didn't fill any medication prescriptions. I was relieved and mad at the same time. I wanted answers, but no answers meant that he still could be alive and well.

CJ made it to Jackie's house before me. I didn't even speak to either one of them. More important things were at hand.

"When's the last time you saw Daddy, Curtis, Jr.?"

"Hello to you, too, Ivory."

"When's the last time you saw Daddy, Curtis, Jr.?"

Just like water, the words flowed out of his mouth. "The day before he went missing. When's the last time *you* saw Daddy?"

"I saw him two days before he went missing. But on the day he went missing, you said that you and Jackie saw him together that day, before he left for his appointment. Which one is it?"

"Ivory, what is this all about?" Jackie asked me.

"Just trying to figure out why CJ and Daddy were arguing in Bangy's restaurant after his appointment the day that he went missing. Just wondering why he followed behind his truck in his car in a rage. Just trying to figure out why he never told us that he saw him that day, after his appointment. Just trying to figure out why he is steady lying, saying that he last saw him the day before he went missing when he saw him the day of, after his appointment! He also said that you and him saw Daddy together before his appointment!"

Jackie's face sank in. "What? CJ, we didn't see him together that day. Why would you say that?"

"Ivory." CJ nervously laughed. "What?"

"Curtis, Jr., I will drag your ass down to Bangy's by them big ass teeth and show you the damn video surveillance myself."

CJ stepped back and scoffed. Jackie and I looked at him until he broke.

"We did meet at Bangy's that day."

"Oh, my God!" Jackie hyperventilated. "Oh, my God! Oh, my God!"

"But, Jackie, I never said anything because we met that day to talk about your Valentine's Day present. I just knew that he would show up that night or the next day with your flowers and new ring and everything else, so I didn't say anything. Then as time went on, I didn't say anything because I knew that would make me look suspicious because I didn't say anything before."

"Still not clear as to why *that day* you didn't say that you saw him *that day*."

"Because I was afraid that y'all would ask what we talked or met about, and I didn't want to let the secret out. I knew I would fold and tell the gifts that he had planned for Jackie. I just knew that he would show up that day or the next day. Jackie. I would never hurt your husband. Ivory. I would never hurt your dad."

"Why did you tell me that you and Jackie saw him together that day?"

"That was my way of letting you know that I did lay my eyes on him that day. I couldn't say I saw him after his appointment because, like I said, I didn't want to reveal what presents he had gotten for Jackie."

"You are such a liar. You had something to do with him going missing. What were you two arguing about?" I asked.

He scoffed over and over. I never backed down. He folded his arms, leaned back, rolled his neck and eyes, and said, "None of your damn business."

"Really? Your freedom and reputation are on the line right now, and that's your answer?" I asked him.

"What me and your dad talked about is none of your business."

"Why do you keep saying *my* dad?"

"Jesus Christ, Ivory. Are you going to be stupid your whole life? Do I look like you or him? Haven't you noticed how everyone is fair skinned, and I'm dark skinned? I don't even look like Mama, so you can't say that I don't look like Daddy because I look like Mama. I look like *my* daddy!"

What the fuck did he just say? Is he drunk? This waste of flesh is always drunk.

Jackie sat down and covered her face.

"Jackie, did you know this? Did you know that Daddy isn't his daddy?!" I asked her.

Jackie just… sat there.

"Okay. You know what, CJ? You are a liar, a drunk alcoholic, a drug addict, and you are trying to distract me. I ain't forgot. You saw Daddy after his appointment and lied about it. And since he ain't your daddy like you claim, it was nothing for you to kill him."

"How the hell can I kill him?!"

"With some kind of chemical. You injected him with something."

"You sound about as crazy as your two different colored eyes look."

"Tell that to the police."

"Police?! What proof do you have?!"

"That ain't my job. The authorities will handle that. You can also explain to them why you drove off behind him in a rage. Y'all have a great day."

"I drove off behind him because that was the way to get to my job! I went to work after we left Bangy's, and he went to whatever wet pussy he could find! I was at work! I have proof of that!"

I walked away. CJ was yelling expletives and inaudibles. I couldn't care less. I had had enough of all of this. And CJ's new sideshow attraction was that he wasn't Daddy's child. He always needed attention, good or bad. He always had to be the star of the show. But I had no time to entertain him that day. Daddy was his daddy, with his lying ass! Anything CJ could say to get a gasp out of someone, he would. CJ lived for the shock factor. Daddy and Mama would have been told me if CJ and I had different daddies. Daddy named him after him for God's sake!

But that was neither here nor there. I needed Daddy to show up dead or alive. My stomach, mind, body, and soul just couldn't take no more. It was time for this to end.

I called the police from my car and told them about CJ and Daddy arguing before his disappearance. They said they would look into it. They had been shit this whole time, so I didn't have much faith that they would be less shitty with this piece of information. But I did what I had to do. That's all I could do. I let it go and gave it to God.

Chapter 11

February 24th, 2020
DAY 11- Monday

This is some hot ass chili. Good, but hot. That's what I get for using that Creole recipe. A northerner like me ain't used to all these spices. All I wanted was some chili for this cold day. Now, my nose running, tongue bur—

"Babe! You okay?!"

I ran from the kitchen table and met my husband Charles at the door after he stormed through it. He had just come in from his daily run. He was bent over, clutching his knees, shirt soaking wet. He ran every day. I mean eight days a week. He never sweated that hard. It was also snowing outside. He had no reason to be sweating that hard.

"Charles, did you take a new route? Ran faster than you usually do?" I asked, while running my hands across his face.

His head remained down as he tried to catch his breath. His chest was heaving, his back was rising and falling. I tried to straighten his back out, but he wouldn't budge. I heard him trying to answer me, but words couldn't make their way out of his mouth.

"I'm calling 911. I'm afraid you're having a heart attack."

As I was turning to run to the phone, he grabbed my shirt, stopping me. That's when he looked up at me. I finally saw his face. He wasn't sweating; he was crying. He stood up and exhaled a breath that I could tell he had been holding in a long time. I backed out of his grasp and said nothing.

Charles was not a crier. He kept all of his emotions in check. He was always cool, calm, and collected. He kept my world together when it was falling apart.

I was horrified. I couldn't speak! I couldn't ask what was wrong. I was terrified of what he might say. But I was even more terrified to walk away not knowing.

"What's wrong, Charles?" I squeaked.

He stooped down, pressed me against his tears-filled shirt, and whispered, "Ivory, they found him. They found your dad."

"You're crying. Why are you crying? You aren't supposed to be crying! Stop crying! Please, don't be crying! Why are you crying?!" I sobbed.

I bent over in agony. I couldn't stop screaming. I couldn't stop crying. I couldn't stop hyperventilating. I couldn't stop! I didn't need him to say it. I already knew.

I already knew.

"Ivory."

"How did you find out? Who found him? Where?"

"CJ called me a few minutes ago. He said he didn't call you because he thought you were at work."

"That motherfucker is lying! I haven't worked on a Monday in years. He is avoiding me!"

"Baby, even if he is, that is not important right now."

"Where was he found?"

"A lady was throwing a baby shower and looked out the window and saw him just sitting up in his truck. She recognized the truck from the news." He paused to wipe his tears. "She said she saw the truck lights flickering on and off, so she walked up to him to see if he was okay. She opened the door and touched him, and that's when she realized he was… cold."

"Where was he? What city? What neighborhood?"

"Near 7 Mile and Woodward."

"What?! We searched there a million times."

"I know, Baby. Somebody obviously put him there."

I called CJ immediately. He told me that he was at the scene. That his body was not decomposed, and the coroner stated that it looked like he had been dead less than ten hours. He told me not to come to the scene because they were about to take him away.

I wanted to see Daddy for myself. I wanted to feel the air surrounding him. I wanted to be there. It wasn't real to me. I needed it to be real. I wouldn't accept it as truth unless I saw it. The body bag. The coroner's van. His hand. Something.

But I didn't go to the scene since they would have taken him away by the time I made it there. It would have taken me about an hour to get there. I stayed home like CJ told me to. When it was all said and done, Jackie said they didn't take Daddy away until about two and a half hours after CJ told me not to come.

I could've gone and seen my daddy.

****

***Tonight's Local News reports body of missing Madison Heights man found inside his truck in Detroit** was the headline of the Breaking News.

The news reporter reported, "The body of a seventy-year-old Madison Heights man missing since February thirteenth was found Monday night on Detroit's east side. Curtis Jones was discovered dead inside his blue Ford pickup truck in the area of 7 Mile and Woodward, relatives report. The family said they hope the cause was medical and not foul play, but no details of the police investigation have been released yet.

"Jones went missing after an appointment. His wife saw him leave and says he appeared normal. Jones left with his cell phone, but the phone had been off since he was reported missing. He checked into the hospital at 1 p.m. for his 1:20 appointment. Police say he checked out at 1:41 p.m. Stay tuned as we follow this story for more."

My daddy was dead.

Chapter 12

Time. Ha! Time. Let me tell you about Time. Time is a funny bitch. She moves slow when you want her to hurry her ass up. And when you want her to slow down, she moves as if there's a fire some damn where. Time lingers; Time evades you. Time is on your side; Time is your worst enemy.

I couldn't find Time. I couldn't find her when I needed to cry. I couldn't find her when I needed to laugh. I couldn't find her when I needed to go to work to keep my mind off things. I couldn't find her when I needed to help Jackie arrange things for the… funeral.

Time was nowhere to be found. But I'll tell you what that bitch Time did allow me to do: nothing and everything at the same damn time. I was just on autopilot. A lot of moving and doing, but no accomplishing. I couldn't find Time to accomplish anything.

I looked up, and it was the day of his… funeral. Time had evaded me just that quickly. My heart was in mourning, my mind was frazzled, I had lost weight that had nothing to do with Weight Watchers, I was weak, and tired of being tired.

I had done well at masking the pain, but I barely had the mental capacity to attend the funeral service that morning because sleep evaded me every single night. On the nights I was able to sleep, my father visited me in my dreams telling me he was sorry. Sorry for what, I didn't know. Every time it was time for him to tell me why he was sorry, I either woke up, or he gave me some bullshit answer.

This hurt was just bad. I didn't know what to think, how to feel, or who I was angry with. I was on autopilot, waiting for the plane to crash. Only Jesus Himself could help get me through this.

The morning of the funeral, I felt like the weight of the world was on my shoulders as I trudged into the church wearing one of my father's fedoras with my head held down. The church was packed to capacity with friends, family, and people I hadn't seen since I was a little girl. As I looked around, I could tell my father was well loved and respected, but even with this elaborate send-off to his proverbial home, it still didn't ease the pain. I remember praying and sobbing, "Lord, please give me strength." I'd heard that prayer a million times before in churches and out and about, and it always seemed so generic and dry and cliché. But I now understood. I literally needed God to give me strength.

The funeral felt like time was moving in slow motion. I don't remember who preached, what songs were sung, or even "who got the body"—the answer that all Black people want to know for some odd reason when people die. But I do remember my husband's speech. I remember it because I wondered how he had the strength or know-how to get up there and flow so eloquently with all the pain that he had experienced. There were times that my husband cried harder and deeper than me. Yet, there he was.

"Curtis and I went suit shopping," my husband began his speech. "While driving to the store, I noticed his suit bags and realized he does not buy his suits off-the-rack. His stuff is custom made. I started thinking, 'I do not have tailor suit money.' I *barely* had shirt, tie, and sock money.

"As he parked the truck, I was dreading going into the store. I wasn't prepared to be embarrassed from how broke I was. Soon as we walked in, all the salespeople were calling his name. He said hi to everyone and then said, 'This is my son-in-law. Treat him real good. Give him that Curtis Jones treatment.'

"They rushed over to meet me and asked what I was looking for. I said the clearance section. They all laughed, but me and my shirt and sock money were serious.

"Curtis started picking out patterns and grabbing ties, so I grabbed a few shirts and ties, and he slapped my hand. I looked like, *No, he didn't just slap my hand.* Then he said, 'You don't match your suit and tie colors. You let them blend and fall into the color.'

"When God was creating the Earth, after each completion, He would say, 'It is good.' That's what I came to tell you today. To everyone that was in Curtis's life, you were not matched with Curtis.

You were blended with him, and the Lord completed his time here on Earth. And today, the Lord is saying, 'It is good.'"

Jackie shocked us all. She was so upbeat, and the words flowed out of her mouth like water. She was able to push past her pain and encourage us.

At one point in the funeral, she asked everyone who ever shopped in Daddy's warehouse to stand up. In a funeral of over four hundred people, at least two hundred people stood up. She called his closet a warehouse because it was packed from top to bottom, left to right with clothes. He had so many clothes that she allowed friends and family to just go in his closet and take what they wanted after he died.

A few days before his funeral, Jackie requested that everyone wear a fedora hat and/or a handkerchief in remembrance of Daddy. Since tradition has it that men aren't supposed to wear hats in church, the women wore fedoras, and the men wore handkerchiefs.

The repast was a joke. The investigation into my father's death was still pending, and my raggedy ass family was at odds for whatever reason. We couldn't even laugh and reminisce about Daddy at his repass because they all had beef with each other for some reason or another. I'm not even sure when that happened, but it happened. I had beef with no one except CJ because I suspected that he had a role in Daddy's death. But everyone else was in discord with everyone else. I obviously missed something when I had checked out of life. My family not getting along with each other was a total shock to me.

I hadn't spoken to CJ other than poor attempts at making funeral arrangements and through the text that he sent informing me and our sisters Rihanna and Honey that the figures from Daddy's estate didn't sit well with him and that he was getting a lawyer. **You're either with me or you're not, and if you're with me, I'll need a thousand dollars from each of you**, CJ's text said. He wasn't even in the ground, and this selfish, money-grubbing sorry excuse of a human being was already talking about lawyering up! I didn't know about Rihanna and Honey's intentions, but I wanted no parts of what CJ was cooking up!

I hadn't even thought about money, beneficiaries, trustees—nothing. All I could think about was how I wanted my daddy back. Period. Nothing else. How could CJ's mind even go there? I spoke to him in passing at the repass. Nothing in particular that I remember talking with him about.

I had no idea that that would be the last time I talked to him.

Chapter 13

CJ died the day of Daddy's funeral. I don't wish to discuss the details. Honestly, the pain from my dad's death was so powerful that I didn't take the time to fully grieve and think about CJ's death. His and my relationship had been strained since childhood. Him not being around anymore felt no different.

When CJ was alive, I couldn't call and talk to him. That was the same narrative in his death. When he was alive, we didn't hang out or take sibling trips. That was no different in his death. When he was alive, I didn't desire his presence. When he died, I didn't wish for it.

I didn't want him back. I didn't pray for it to be a nightmare that I would wake up from. I just let him go. I allowed him to rest in peace.

And my life was so much more peaceful without him in it. He was always intoxicated and causing a scene. There was always drama following him. If his life was too quiet, you better believe he was going to make some noise. If there was peace, you could bet on him causing hell.

While I didn't miss his presence or want him back, I did wish that things were different between us before he left. I wished that I could have gone through Daddy's death with CJ. I wished that he would have gone through it with me.

I wished that we had that relationship to lean on each other. To be the other's balance. Where one was weak, it would have been great that the other was strong. Where one was leaning, it would have been refreshing that the other one propped the other up. But that just wasn't how we ever functioned.

It was just like his selfish ass to disappear right when I needed him the most. So typical of him to not fight to remain in my life and just leave me to figure out how to breathe without Daddy. Just like him to add to the pot of sorrow, misery, and reminiscence. I wished that CJ would have fought to stay. Not because I wanted him around per se, but I wanted him to want to be here. He didn't fight to stay at all. He allowed himself to be removed, as if he was never here.

I wished that we had a true sibling bond that I could sit up and reflect on. Up until my twenties, there were so many days and nights that I prayed for God to soften his heart and love me. "Lord, please turn his stony heart into a pillow. Allow his heart to bleed for me," was the last prayer I prayed over our relationship.

God didn't answer that prayer. I asked Him a lot of times why He wouldn't allow him to like me, want me around, desire my presence. God told me, "You often pray for me to protect you. Keeping him away from you is your protection."

I told Que what God said to me, and she said, "You don't know the evil that CJ is capable of. If God said you need protection from him, you need protection from him. Don't go digging and find out why CJ isn't safe."

I took her advice. I left it alone. I was in my twenties before I accepted that CJ wasn't for me or good for me. I just wish that wasn't the truth. Some other people's siblings have a close bond and are their protectors. He was my damn Kryptonite.

I already didn't have a good relationship with my mom. Having a brother that I could vent to and laugh with would have eased that pain. What a joy it would have been to stay on the phone all night with CJ while Charles huffed and puffed, waiting on me to get off the phone with him and give him some.

It never happened. And it never will. He was now dead. Gone. Never to return. That was the end. I prayed that he went to hell because even though I couldn't prove it, I know he had something to do with Daddy's death. Now that he was dead, I would never get to the bottom of that. I would never get my answers. I pray he is getting what he deserves.

May he rest in shit.

Chapter 14

Jackie was still the best other mother I could have ever asked for. My dad being gone didn't change our relationship. It didn't change the memories or all that she had done for me ever since I was a preteen. I always made it my business to hang out with her in some capacity at least once a week.

One day, about a month after Dad's passing, I was at Jackie's house, and her friend Ms. Victoria was there visiting with some of Jackie's other friends. The conversation of my dad came up. I was in and out of the conversation because my dad was still such a sore topic for me. I didn't know if I missed him, was angry at him, hated him, or all the above. But what did catch my attention was when Ms. Victoria said, "Curtis did a lot of things. But one thing he did do right was be a great dad to a child that wasn't his."

I looked up and asked her, "Who was he a dad to?"

The entire room went quiet for a few seconds. There was some nervous laughter. Other people avoided eye contact with me. Jackie said nothing.

"Girl, you're so funny!" Ms. Victoria eventually said to me.

I'm sure I looked like a deer in headlights.

"Y'all ready to eat?" Jackie asked, attempting to change the subject.

"Who was he a daddy to?" I asked Ms. Victoria again.

"Curtis, Jr.," she answered, as a matter-of-factly. "Curtis was not his dad. As different as he looked, you didn't pick up on that? Curtis, Jr. knew it. His friends knew it. Jackie knew it. Your whole family knows it. Everybody in this room knows it. Your mama damn sure knows it. You didn't know? How the hell you don't know?!"

My heart leaped up through my throat and down to my feet. Whatever my face said made everybody else in the entire room say nothing else for the rest of the visit. How the hell did literally everyone know but me? People who weren't even in my family. The neighbors. The co-workers. *Everybody*. Everybody, except Ivory.

Why would my parents deceive me my entire life? Why keep that from me but tell everyone else? How did it skip me? How had I not heard it through the grapevine before my forties? CJ told me that when Daddy was missing, but I ignored his lying, drunk, high ass. But that was actually the one time he told the truth.

"Jackie, is this the truth?" I asked her.

Jackie looked at me and said nothing. I know she was trying to be respectful to my parents and say nothing, but I needed answers. I wanted to know the truth.

"Baby, you have to ask your mom. I never saw any blood test confirming or denying it, but your mama was pregnant before she even met your daddy. She thinks nobody knows, but everybody knows," Ms. Victoria said. "Call her and ask her, Ivory. She'll tell you. She can't deny what everybody knows."

I didn't even bother asking my mom about it that day. All she was going to do was lie and play victim. Charles' response was, "That doesn't change the fact that your dad was a great dad to you. You wanted for nothing. You lacked nothing. You're already missing him. He already left his after-death business in a mess. You don't need to add anything else to what you're feeling. Him not being CJ's dad has nothing to do with you. It's nothing to take personal. That's between him, CJ, and your mama. That situation is not your assignment. Don't stress out behind that. Love and remember your dad for who he was."

But I took it personal. I took it hella personal. It cut deep. Did they not trust my reaction? Like I would love CJ any less? Did my parents think I would look at them differently? Did they think I couldn't handle the truth? Why was I kept in the dark when they shined a light on it for the rest of the world?

And my dad was dead. I couldn't approach him about it. I couldn't get a better understanding. There would be no closure from this. It was something else added to the pot of "deal with it and move on."

But that pot was boiling over.

Chapter 15

"Ivory, I got the turkey chops—" Charles' words were stifled in his throat when he laid his eyes on my naked body.

It was all or nothing at all. I was propped up on my elbows in the middle of the bed, one leg in Utah, the other leg in New York. He dropped his keys and quickly swallowed the saliva that was attempting to make its way out of his mouth.

"Bae, you okay?" he asked me.

Wasn't the reaction I was expecting, but I kept it moving.

"No." I pouted. I placed my right middle and ring fingers in my mouth, sucked them slowly, and placed them on my clitoris. I went in circles, up and down, side to side, throwing my head back in ecstasy that I wasn't experiencing.

He stood in the room, cemented to the floor, watching me. It still wasn't the reaction that I was expecting, but I kept it moving.

"Sssss," I moaned. "Aaaah!" I squealed. "Mmmm," I groaned.

He walked towards me, hovered over me, and placed my right middle and ring fingers in his mouth.

"You sure?" he whispered.

"Yes."

He placed both of my arms over my head as he explored every inch of my body. There was no place that his tongue and hands didn't go.

And I was as dry as a desert.

Images of my daddy in the casket overtook my mind, and I couldn't shake it.

Think about your favorite porn scene. Think about your sexual fantasy. Hell! Think about ice cream! Get it together, Ivory, I silently fussed at myself.

His tongue met my sensitive button… all for me to find out that it wasn't sensitive anymore. He was putting in his best work, and I had no moisture to give him.

"Ivory, we can just—"

"NO! Lay down."

I didn't want to hear him say that we could "just talk" or "just watch TV" or "just go to sleep." I wanted to fuck, and that's exactly what we were going to do.

"Lay down!" I repeated myself.

He hesitantly laid down on his back. I mounted him and tried my best to think lustful thoughts.

"Ivory—"

"Shut up, Charles! Just let me do this."

I kissed him on his lips. He kissed me with more passion than I had to offer. He held my hips tight. I'm not sure if it was to stop me from trying to do anything else, or if he was caressing me, but I removed his hands and began to move south.

He was standing at attention for me. It had been so long since I saw it that it almost scared me. I've never wanted something so bad while not wanting it at all.

I guided it into my mouth and allowed the suction to control the movements.

My mouth was also a desert.

"Bae—" he began, with sorrow.

"No! Just stick it in me!"

I got on all fours in the bed. He didn't move. He just stared at me.

"Come on, Charles! Fuck me!"

"Bae. Just—"

"Fuck. Me. Why are you making me beg for it?!"

"Ivory. You are too dry. I will hurt you if I try to penetrate you."

"Go get the KY!"

"Or we can—"

"Or you can just leave me the hell alone!"

"I will not," he calmly said. "Not ever. So you can just get that out of your head right now."

I got off of all fours and fell to my stomach. "Please," I whimpered.

"No," he stated, as a matter-of-factly.

There was complete silence in the room. I couldn't even hear my own thoughts. He turned me over onto my back and placed me on his chest.

"I miss my daddy!" I belted out.

"I miss him, too, Ivory. Lord knows I do. You're supposed to miss him. It's only been three months. And your brother is gone, too. It's rough right now. And you and I haven't spoken about it, but your mom may not be around much longer, either. I know she's always on your mind. It's all over your face. You're moving too fast. Just give it time."

"I'm not even a decent lay. I can't give a proper blowjob. I can't even please *myself*! I am just worthless."

"It's just for this season, Ivory. This isn't forever. You have my word that it won't always be like this. You gone be bending it over, busting it wide open, throwing it back, and choking on this tree trunk soon. Just not today. Give yourself time. Black Licorice ain't going nowhere."

"Black Licorice? What is that?"

"Me!"

I laughed out loud. "Where the hell calling yourself Black Licorice come from?"

" 'Cause I'm so nasty."

"Boy!" I playfully hit him and laid my head on his neck. "Chitterlings ain't going nowhere, either."

"Chitterlings?!" he hollered while laughing. "It fits you 'cause you are full of shit!"

"Shut up, Charles!"

"At least I didn't say you *smell* like shit."

I tried to laugh, smile, giggle, chuckle, something. But the emotions came out of nowhere, and tears flooded my face.

"Thank you for being my rock, Charles."

"I'm only doing it for pussy."

"Lies!"

"What? You thought I loved you? Girl, naw. I just don't wanna be dipping in something that's gonna burn when I dip out. You a clean girl. I ain't gotta worry about laying up with you."

"Joke's on you because I been having discharge all day. I just wasn't going to say nothing."

"Who don't like a little sour cream on their taco?"

"You are disgusting!" I laughed.

"Black Licorice, Baby."

Chapter 16

After literally being locked in the house for nearly a year due to the pandemic, we were approaching the first Christmas without my father. I knew my stepmother was struggling emotionally. There were no words to console her, but I wanted to give her a gift to show her that she was not alone. I too was feeling the emptiness of the holiday season, but she had lost her best friend. She had gone from having a small army of people at her house to no one besides the dog, her shadow, and bad dreams. And to top it off, she had packed up years of her life, her marriage, and the mess Daddy left behind after his death to downsize from a twenty-eight hundred square foot house to a much smaller condo. Although I prayed for her every single day and talked to her every morning, I wanted to get her a thoughtful gift to remind her that she was in my thoughts and prayers.

After racking my brain on what I could get my stepmother, the voicemails that I had saved from my father came to mind. It was extremely close to Christmas, but I had enough time to get it done and get it to her so she'd have something to open for Christmas. I got up super early so I could make it to the mall before the crowd. I found the Build-A-Bear kiosk and put my father's recorded voice from voicemails saying, "I LOVE YOU" in a couple of little teddy bears: one for me and one for Jackie.

Grief was a normal process. I'd been through all the phases multiple times over this year. I had no idea that Build-A-Bear was gonna be such an emotional process. First, you have to get the volume and exactness of the recording to your liking. Then they give you a little felt heart, ask you to close your eyes, rub it, and make a wish. Thank God my daughter and I were the only ones at the kiosk because I stood there crying like a newborn baby. Cleansing my soul and grieving my first Christmas without my father in the middle of the mall was a new overwhelming feeling for me.

Most days, I was good. But, damn, I missed my daddy. When the tears dried up, I had secured the perfect gift, and now I have the pleasure of hearing his voice and the memories of him saying, "I LOVE YOU" at the press of my fingertips.

When I gave Jackie the bear for Christmas, you would have thought that I had given her a Maserati. She hugged the bear with all her might. She pressed the button over and over, not allowing time for the bear to finish his statement. She kissed the bear time after time and drowned it with her tears.

Christmas wasn't the same without Daddy, but at least his voice was there. If only I could have had his voice to guide me through other things in life, like my first birthday without him, first Thanksgiving without him, even my first period without him. My cramps were no joke. I know he would've told inappropriate jokes about clots, pregnancy, and menopause to ease my pain.

Just being without him had by far been one of the hardest times of my life. The only harder time was when my eleven-month-old son died. To accompany one of the hardest times of my life was it also being my first year without my mom.

My first Christmas without my mom.

I knew that she was slipping away. I tried with all my might to hold on to her, but she was so determined to go. I could hear it in her voice and see it in her eyes that she could no longer stay. It had gotten to the point that it hurt me more to try to keep her here with me than it did to accept the truth and let her go. Truth be told, I stand firm on my belief that she and CJ are together, raising hell, giving Lucifer a challenge.

Even with there being a pandemic, and people dying suddenly, everyone in my family was still at odds with each other. If anyone talked to anyone, we had to apologize to someone about it. "I'm sorry Cousin Nikki that I texted 'Happy birthday' to Aunt Bea." "I'm sorry Uncle Harry that I called Uncle Roy when his wife died." It was insane.

So, I had to go through my first year without my dad—and brother and mom— alone. I didn't have family to comfort me or lean on, and it was starting to take a toll on my mental. The few friends that I did have, I couldn't really spend time with because COVID-19 had everyone so scared to even wave at each other. Staying apart was supposed to keep us alive, but the separation was actually killing people.

I could hardly sleep at night, and when I was awake, often my mind drifted. I'd been so immersed in everything that was going on with this pandemic that I wasn't able to fully give in to my own grief. I was just a robot, surviving off of routine: get up, pray, go to work, go home, eat, try to be a good mom, sleep, and repeat.

Most days I felt like a ticking time bomb. Every day I woke up telling myself, "Today is a new day, a new beginning. I'm going to start fresh with positive thoughts and work hard to keep my emotions in check." And every day it was a challenge to not go back to that ugly place of affliction.

Over the next several months, as holidays and birthdays passed, I found that the check-ins from friends and family became less frequent. People tell you things like, "Be strong." "Keep your head up." "Pray and it'll get better as time goes on." "He's in a better place now." "She's looking down, so proud of you."

I feel like some people think there's supposed to be a time frame on how long you grieve a loss. They didn't really care to hear that one year later, I was still struggling with the loss of my father, my mother, and in a strange way, my brother. They just wanted to check off a box to make themselves feel better for checking in on me. But the truth of the matter is I had been so immersed with everything that was going on with this pandemic that I hadn't really been able to fully grieve, and the result was me walking around angry, short witted, and lashing out at those close to me.

The autopsy revealed that a heart attack is what killed my dad. Nothing alarming was found in his system. I'm not denying a heart attack. But I never found out what led him to have a heart attack. Why was he missing all those days? What was going on then?

When they found him on the eleventh day of him being missing, he had been dead for less than ten hours. So he had recently had the heart attack. I heard that Freon causes a heart attack and is undetectable on an autopsy. I never Googled it to find out if that's true or not. I don't want to know that bad. It may make the pain worse to know that someone killed my dad with Freon.

I spent a lot of time thinking about how my daughter Mychaela isn't close with any of her cousins, so it made me worry about her future. One day my husband and I will be gone, and there will be no family left for my daughter. I sat and thought a lot about that.

About a year after my brother died, I went to have my annual mammogram screening and some blood drawn for thyroid testing. While filling out the health forms, I came to the section on breast cancer family history. While I'd known that some males and females on my mother's side had been diagnosed with breast cancer at some point in time, I could only guestimate their ages of when they were diagnosed. A sadness washed over me that I had no factual ages, and with everyone gone, there was not one single soul I could go to for answers.

I wished I could just pick up the phone and call my mother. Not only because I wanted to know my family's health history, but I was also scared and nervous. At that moment, I needed my mommy. I wanted my mother to tell me not to worry about the results of the tests and everything was gonna be alright, but sadly, that was never gonna happen, even if she had been alive. I could never call on my mom for consolation. She was never nurturing, caring, or loving. Me being afraid that I had cancer wasn't going to change that.

A couple of weeks after my mammogram, I found a breast cancer awareness calendar where CJ had done a photo shoot. According to the blurb in the calendar, I learned that at the age of forty-five during a routine yearly mammogram, there were changes detected in his right breast. The doctor was unable to feel anything, so a biopsy was performed. He was diagnosed with (DCIS) Ductal Carcinoma in Situ stage 0, which is the most common type of noninvasive breast cancer. Had it not been for the information in the calendar, I wouldn't have known any of this.

All of my tests came out with favorable results. Thank God because I couldn't handle my world falling any more apart than it already was. I was on a slow countdown to losing my mind. The clock of my remaining sanity was ticking second by second.

That clock eventually struck midnight.

Chapter 17

September 2021

"I'm so glad to see you, Ivory. I am Dr. Elodie Mable. Please, have a seat."

I finally went to a therapist like my husband and Que had been begging me to. I was there. I did what I said I would do. I went. I never said that I would talk.

Dr. Mable called herself an unconventional therapist. Even prided herself in it from what I could see. Supposedly, she had great results by the reviews I had heard.

Sure. I went. Why not?

"I wish I could say that I'm glad to be here. But I'm not."

"You see my bright, beautiful, gorgeous, sunshine face, and you're not glad to be here? What else do you need?" she asked.

I guess she was trying to be funny. Lightening up the mood, I'm assuming, was her angle. But nah. It wasn't working. That shit didn't work on me. I wasn't so simple minded that a poorly executed mood softener would make me break down and open up to a stranger.

"What else do I need?" I asked, repeating her question back to her. "I need my daddy back."

"Your dad," she said, reading notes off of a piece of paper, "passed away a little over a year and a half ago from a heart attack."

"Yes."

"And according to the questionnaire you filled out, your brother passed away the day of your dad's funeral, and your mom died roughly seven months after your brother?"

"Yes."

"I am so sorry. You lost both your parents and a sibling in under one year. That is heart-wrenching. Probably to the point that you want to bitch slap somebody, but you don't know who."

"I would start with my brother Curtis, Jr."

"Is he the one who died?"

"Yes. We call him CJ."

"You would slap him for dying?"

"I don't need a reason for slapping that bitch," I growled. "Or my mama."

"Spill the tea, Sis!"

"Hell. I don't even know where to start. I'm so angry at them! We never had a good relationship. Never! I just knew that we would one day have that relationship that I dreamed of. Sibling trips. Mommy-Daughter dates. Just lying in each other's beds just because. They had the nerve to die before we could get it right."

"How did they die?"

"My brother—." I paused. "My mom—."

I couldn't talk about it. I wanted to. I really did. But I couldn't. The pain of them being gone was more so from the pain of when they were present. I missed them… but I didn't. I wanted them back… but I was relieved they were gone. The conflicting feelings were more painful than them not being here. I can't explain the emotions. I never was able to navigate them. My dad's death was more important, and I hadn't healed from that, yet. Everything else was just going to have to wait.

"You don't have to answer. Not right now. We have plenty of time to talk about your brother and mom. What about your dad? Can you talk about him?"

I felt my face immediately glow. Then it went dark as quickly as it glowed. As much as I loved my daddy, I hated the truth about him: he was a lying, secretive, deceiving whore.

"I see the confliction on your face. Let me guess. You loved a pink monster. He was sweet, lying, gentle, cheating, present, manipulating, loving, secretive."

I chuckled at the truth. "As far as I can remember, I have always been a daddy's girl," I began. "Even as an adult, every time I saw my dad, I would run up to him, give him a big kiss, tickle him, and tell him it was selfie time. He loved selfies. Selfie time resulted in us taking many selfies in different poses. Duck lips, silly poses, mean faces. Over the years, we must've taken well over one thousand selfies. All of which I still have.

"I'm the second oldest of four and a rumored younger brother who I've only seen baby pictures of. He supposedly is ten years younger than me. Growing up, I only knew it to be my brother CJ and me. It wasn't until I was in my early thirties that we learned that there was a sister named Rihanna that was just ten months younger than me. Learning that I had another sibling brought about so many emotions. I went from being upset to thinking maybe this was God's way of giving me a second chance at having a sibling to build a loving relationship with.

"My stepmother gave me her number. I called Rihanna, and we agreed that she would come over my house to meet for the first time. You see, all her life, her mother had been telling her that her father was dead, so she hadn't even met my father, yet. When I met her, I was blown away! She looked a lot like our daddy and a lot like me. We even had the exact same tattoo in the exact same spot! This was surreal!

"All these years of thinking her father was dead, she had no idea what her father looked like! Not having seen a picture of our father, I pulled out a few photo album books, introduced her to pictures of a family she never knew existed, and told her, 'Ask me whatever you want to know.'

"Daddy was one of the biggest liars that I knew, so I knew I should've had a face-to-face conversation so I could look him in his eyes when I asked him about her, but I couldn't wait. Although I could look at my newfound sister and see that she was damn near the spitting image of both me and my daddy, I had to allow him the opportunity to tell the truth. I wanted to hear his side of the story.

"I called my daddy on the phone to ask him about this illegitimate daughter who looks just like me, and at first, he flat out denied her. 'No!' he said. 'The only kids that I have are you and Curtis, Jr.'

"I remember being filled with so much hurt, anger, and disappointment that I cried until I realized this could be the sibling bond that I'd been missing. Although I had accepted her, Daddy still was denying her, so I hadn't quite processed it, yet. I still was thinking about CJ being my only sibling.

"It wasn't until weeks later when my stepmother confirmed what I already knew. She showed me the blood test results of him being Rihanna's daddy and back child support payments that Daddy had been paying for years. Daddy finally came clean after I showed him the proof, and boy was my mother on fire! My mother and father were in the midst of a divorce when I was conceived, so she was livid to find out he had made another baby while still married to her. She instantly hated my new sister.

"About five years after learning about Sister Rihanna, we found out that we had another sister named Honey. Although we knew nothing about her, Daddy knew all about her. Her mother lived down the street from my grandfather who my father took care of. When I first laid eyes on her, I thought she was the spitting image of my father's oldest sister."

I paused to shift gears. Enough of that. It was already done. On to happy thoughts.

"My father called me weekly," I continued. "Depending on where I was, I would let the call go to voicemail. You see, Daddy had a stroke in the late nineties which left him partially paralyzed on his right side and with a speech and hearing impairment. So, when he called, I had to make sure there was no background noise surrounding me so I could try to make out what it was that he was saying. If you asked him to repeat himself too many times, he'd get frustrated and shut down.

"Anyway, I say all this to say, at the end of every phone voicemail that he left me, he'd say, 'I LOVE YOU! I LOVE YOU! I-VO-REEEE! THIS IS YOUR FATHER.' Like I didn't know who he was." I laughed to myself. "I didn't know at the time that these voicemails would be something that I'd cherish dearly. I listen to them quite often.

"I'm mad at my father for dying and leaving us with such a big ass mess! His affairs were just not in order when he died, which only further separated the family. I'm mad that he treated his wife Jackie like shit and bad-mouthed her so much that people treat her like a villain rather than the grieving widow that she is. She cared for him. She cooked, cleaned, took care of their business, cleaned up shit and wiped his ass when he couldn't wipe it for himself. She did everything that no one else was willing to do. And even in death, she's still cleaning up his shit.

"No, my father was not a monster. He just wasn't an angel.

"I also hurt for my daughter Mychaela. He was at every swim meet of hers, cheering her on big time! And I mean *every*. I always knew to look for him in the bleachers. Sometimes, he would beat me there.

"Rain or shine, he never missed a SIDS Walk for Javaughn. Javaughn is my son who passed away when he was eleven months old. My dad was the biggest supporter I had during that time.

"His grandkids could pretty much talk him into giving them anything if they asked sweet enough. Mychaela was the only one of the little kids who wasn't scared of him. With his big eyebrows and big full beard, he may have looked like a grizzly bear, but he was all teddy when it came to his grandkids.

"And God took him away from his grandkids. God took him away from me! I know I'm rambling and all over the place, but God went too far when He took my daddy."

"Are you angry with God for your father, mother, and brother passing away?"

"DAMN RIGHT I'M ANGRY! You don't think I have the right to be angry? Death changes the living! Why would God take my father, my mother, and my brother? Although my mother never wanted me and made sure to often remind me of that fact; and although the only sibling that I knew of growing up hated me for being born, I still loved them both. Regardless of how they shut me out, I still tried to be a good daughter and sister. They were my family. They were the only family I had left on my mother's side of the family. Why?! Is God punishing me for something I did in the past? Why would He leave me all alone?

"I literally have no one on my mom's side who I can call and talk to. Call and express my feelings. Just go walk the mall with. And I've never really had a great relationship with anyone on my dad's side. Even though I never really had my mama and brother, at least they were accessible. They were within arm's reach. Now, they're not even that. It's just me.

"I don't want to keep crying to my husband. I know he would listen every time. But at some point, you get tired of whining. At some point, you get tired of complaining about the same thing to the same people. I guess that's why I agreed to come to see you. A new ear to hear my shit. A new ear to hear what God did to me. You think I'm crazy, don't you?"

"No, I don't. I think you have the wrong perception. Ivory, you are old enough to know that everyone dies. And if God waited on us to say when is a good time for Him to call someone home, very few people would die. The Bible says that when we were in our mother's womb, He knew us. That means that a death date was set before we ever saw the light of day. The Bible says that our spirits will return to God.

"My point is everyone dies. Why would you believe God is punishing you? Do you really believe He would single you out to punish you by taking your family? What makes you think that you are that special?

"Do you feel guilty about something that leads you to believe you should be punished? Help me to understand why you are angry with God, and then we can work on ways you can start to release some of that anger. Prayerfully, that will lead you on a path to restore your faith in God."

"I'm just angry. He wasn't supposed to die."

"You are a deacon's wife. You know that people die every minute. We have to be released from this hell called life and be restored back unto the Father. That's not fair that you wanted your dad to be here forever. Do *you* want to be here forever? Always worrying about bills, sicknesses, health going to shit. Battling all kinds of mental and emotional wars. Don't you want an end date to this bullshit?

"Here's the thing about anger. When you're angry, you're just a character in somebody else's story. But when you let your anger go, you reclaim your own story. You become your own protagonist again. So, let's start at the beginning. You've told me why you're angry, but tell me what lead you to come see me. Because you have been dodging me for a little while. What made you give in?

Obviously, you don't want to keep feeling like this."

"Sometimes, I feel like I'm losing it! I've tried everything! I've prayed about it, tried talking about it, not talking about it, and prayed some more, but nothing I've tried is working. Sometimes, I feel fine, but more than often, I feel like a ticking time bomb. My temper is short, and my patience is as close to gone as gone can be. Since I've tried everything, and nothing helped, you are the last resort."

"Well, don't I feel special. Did all this start with your dad's death?"

"No. It all started less than two years ago. On February 13th, 2020, my father Curtis went to his doctor's appointment in Detroit never to be seen alive again. For eleven excruciating days, my family and friends sat on pins and needles as my daddy's face and blue Ford pickup truck were plastered all over the news and social media. I felt like I was trapped in a nightmare.

"For eleven days, I went to work wearing a mask of smiles without telling a soul the agony that my family was experiencing. Thank God my coworkers didn't watch the news; I never had to answer any of their questions or talk about it. Somehow, I felt like if I talked about it, that would make it real. So, I held it in, prayed, and prayed some more only for my prayers to come back denied.

"All these scriptures about asking and we shall receive. All these stories in the Bible about how God granted people the desires of their hearts. I know people who don't even believe in God, but God hasn't taken their parents and siblings. Now do you see why I'm angry with God?!"

"Yes, I do, Ivory. I hear you. Loud and clear. But the scriptures also tell us that rain falls on the just and unjust. Anybody can get it. We aren't off-limits just because we pray. We all get a turn at happiness; we all get a turn at sorrow. It was just your turn, Baby Girl."

"Then why the fuck am I a Christian then? What are the damn membership perks?!"

"That when we suffer, we don't suffer long. That we have hope because He is hope. That it is not the end. That He will give us the strength to keep going. Our thoughts and emotions won't undertake us. We don't have to become slaves to the pain and anger.

"Ivory, you're going to feel this. Even Jesus wept. If Jesus wasn't immune, you and I surely aren't immune. If Jesus cried, surely, you and I are going to cry. But keep coming here, and just like Jesus, you will rise again."

Chapter 18

"You went to therapy today. I'm so proud of you! Go, Best Friend! That's my best friend!" Que chanted, while trying her best to twerk. Girl couldn't find a rhythm if it had a GPS on it.

"I did. It was pretty much an introduction, I guess. No breakthroughs or nothing. Just getting acquainted with each other. I did a whole lot of rambling with no direction."

"That's fine. You went. At least you talked. You said you would go and not say anything. And that's good that she just let you rant. When do you go back?"

I paused and thought about it. I hadn't considered going back. It wasn't mandatory or anything. I shifted my body weight on the couch. The living room's air was becoming thick.

"It felt good to just talk, right, Ivy? I mean, that is what your short self do best. All your four-foot-eleven ass do is bump your gums."

"I am four eleven and a half!"

"You act like that half is a whole inch."

"And a half!" I repeated.

"Still ain't five feet."

"And a half!"

"My God! And a half!" She laughed.

"As you were saying." I motioned for her to continue in conversation where she left off.

"All yo' li'l ass do is run your mouth. Go run your mouth some more with the therapist. What is his or her name?"

"She's a Black female. Doctor Elodie Mable."

"Elodie?! What kind of name is that? Does she go back to the plantation after this? Does Massa know she leaving the premises? Does Massa know she can'sa read?!"

I laid my head on the end table and tried my best to control my laughter. "I think she's from a different country, Idiot!"

"You know what? I trust ole Stable Mable. She sounds sturdy. Like she can carry a lot of shit on her back and not break. Like she was built to last."

"Que, that's racist."

"I said *nothing* about her race. Ain't she Black like me? I also said nothing about her culture. I was talking about that backwoods name. It has a nice ring to it, though. As a matter of fact, we sang about her last night at Bible Study. 'Don't give up on God 'cause He won't give up on you. He's MABLE!' "

"Quantavia, you're done! You're done!"

"Elodies from heaven, rain down on me! Rain down on me!" she sang.

"I'm not going to hell with you, Que."

"Elodie and Ivory live together in perfect harmony," she continued to sing.

I laughed into my hand. "I will not with you. Not today."

"My name is Quantavia. I got the nerve to talk about somebody's name," she said, once she stopped laughing.

"Exactly. Your name is unique just like hers."

"My name is hood! I don't care what cute stories my parents try to conjure up as to why they named me Quantavia. It doesn't change the fact that they didn't name me Susan Jane."

"Susan Jane is boring. It definitely doesn't match your personality. Susan Jane don't be twerking in public. Susan Jane doesn't even sound like she can cook greens. Susan Jane surely can't retwist my locs!"

"I don't care about none of that. I wouldn't have to teach people how to say Susan Jane thirteen times a day. I sound like a Hooked on Phonics teacher when I'm teaching people how to pronounce my name. 'Take your time. The 'Q' and 'u' together says 'kwuh'. The 'a' and 'n' is 'un', like 'sun'. 'Quan' rhymes with 'sun'. The 'a' after the 't' is long sounding..."

"Girl, stop. If White Americans learned how to say the Russian musical composer's name Tchaikovsky, they damn sure can learn how to say Quantavia. And make them say it right *every time*! No, they can't call you Que for short. They can call you Quantavia."

"Period, Pooh."

"Periodt! Quantavia means 'a beautiful young lady who strives for nothing but greatness! A beautiful friend and listener.' Your mom knew what she was doing when she named you that. You have lived up to every aspect and definition of your name. Your name is as beautiful as you. And as rare as you. You don't find a you every day. That's for damn sure."

Que grabbed my hand. "Ivory. I know this is a hard season for you. Losing both your parents and really the only sibling you've ever really known. And you've lost a lot because of that. But even in the middle of all this, you've still been present in my and my daughter's lives. You still haven't missed a beat. You still have held me down and been one of my favorite people in the world. I mean this from the bottom of my heart: thank you for being a friend. We *will* get through this. Together. Keep going to therapy. And I will keep holding your hand every step of the way. Remember, we're in this thang together 'til the wheels fall off. I love you to the grave and beyond."

"Quantavia. You have my word that I'm going back."

Chapter 19

"You came back!" Dr. Mable squealed, clapping.

"Really? Is all that necessary?"

"Well, unlike you, I am happy that you are here. I really thought you wouldn't come back. It's obvious that you don't like me."

"I guess that's why I came back. It's easier to vent to someone that I can't stand."

"You have said nothing but the truth. Have a seat, please."

I sat on the chaise lounge. Or should I say, I *lounged* on the chaise lounge. Had to be memory foam or something. Damn. With this type of material, who wouldn't spill their guts?"

"Last time, you talked about your dad, mom, and brother. Can you tell me of a happy childhood memory that includes your mother, father, and brother as a family?"

"Well, there aren't many childhood memories that I have that include us all as a family. Growing up, my father never lived in the house with us. I'm told that I was conceived while my parents were in the midst of a divorce. Come to find out, there were a few more kids that were conceived by different women during that divorce, but I've already brushed up on that with you.

"Growing up, I do remember the last weekend of every month, Daddy would come to get my brother CJ and me from our house on the east side of Detroit so we could spend the weekend at his house. Those were times that I would get excited about.

"You see, Daddy had this big presence. He drove a beautiful pink champagne-colored Mark IV with burgundy leather interior. He was always draped in expensive gold jewelry, wore fancy suits with monogrammed dress shirts, and always had a fresh lineup. He had a mouth full of pearly white teeth that could light up a room.

"I would look at him and find it hard to imagine him and my mother together as a couple. With a caramel complexion, round pie face, and flat button nose, Mama Luna is now an average-looking woman. But in her heyday, she was cute and shaped like an hourglass with a big ole booty that looked like two basketballs. Most women envied her shape, and men couldn't stop staring. Now that I'm saying it out loud, I take that back. I see what attracted my father to her. She used to get dolled up back then, but in her older years, aside from her lipstick and fingernails, she didn't put much effort into her looks.

"I remember she used to chain smoke Virginia Slims menthol cigarettes like a chimney. She would let me and my brother twist the tobacco out of the cigarette, and she would fill it with weed and twist it on the end so that the weed stayed in. She also gambled and cussed like a sailor. Daddy didn't do any of those things which was another reason that made it hard to imagine that she wasn't supposed to be nothing more than a quick hit.

"I'm getting off track. Let me get back to the happy. Daddy would come over on the last weekend of the month to get me and my brother and take us to the mall. He would be looking all dapper in his Mark IV with his custom suit, monogrammed shirts, and gold jewelry. We felt like celebrities when he would come to pick us up.

"From the time we set foot in the mall, Daddy told us, 'Don't worry about the cost. You have one hour to get whatever it is that you want.' Man, you should have seen me and CJ running from store to store trying to get any and everything that we wanted. Although I was too young for most of the clothing and shoe stores in Northland Mall that CJ would drag me to, I went along with the promise that he would bring our stuff back to the store and return it for a cash refund. If he ever returned the stuff or not, I don't know, but I know I never got a dime back.

"After we wrapped up our hour-long shopping spree, the rest of the time we'd spend shopping with Daddy in men's clothing stores and him showing us off to all of his friends. All of his friends raved over how much I was the spitting image of my father and laughed and whispered, 'That other one, not so much.'

"I remember we'd go back home full of energy and excited to show Mama all the new stuff that Daddy bought us only to have Mama yell in my face, 'I don't want to see that shit! That shit don't mean shit! If he wants to do something, he needs to pay his child support!' You see, from the top of my head to my butterscotch skin complexion, hazel eyes, luscious lips, and curly toes, I really was the spitting image of my daddy. So much so that my mama couldn't stand the sight of me when he made her mad.

"I see you writing something. What are you writing? I know I'm just rambling, but I guess this is where my happy memories start."

"I write the things that jump out at me. Questions for later. Concerns. Things like that."

"What concerns do you have?"

"Your relation*shit* you had with your mom."

That made me chuckle. That's exactly what it was. A relation*shit.*

"What concerns you about our relationshit?"

"Hell. Everything that came out of your mouth, honestly. Sounds like you had a dysfunctional relationship with all three of them. Sounds like your dad tried to buy you, your brother used you, and your mom neglected you. I'm not sure I hear real love in any of these relationshits."

"Well, my dad did love me! You can't have two sessions with me and just jump to those conclusions. You asked about a happy memory. I answered your question."

"Your happy memory is your dad buying your love?"

"Like I said. I pulled out *one* memory. I had forty-six years with my dad. I have a million that don't involve money.

"One of the memories that I hold near and dear to me is when my son was in the hospital from birth to seven months old. My dad went to see my son Javaughn often. He sat with us, cracked jokes, and sometimes just sat in silence. But just to have him there with me, with us, was all that we needed.

"I remember Javaughn coded on the day of my stepmom's dad's funeral—my dad's father-in-law. My father was at the hospital before me. He chose my son that day. We didn't think my son was gonna make it, but the doctors were able to revive him. I can't tell you how much that meant to have my daddy there. He made sure I wasn't alone during the most painful, agonizing time of my life.

"And he made sure that I was never alone during the best times of my life, too. My dad always made sure I wasn't alone. And he always came back for me. *Always.* I can't believe he didn't come back for me this last time. I can't believe he had the audacity to die!"

I cried into my hands. That day I woke up and said I wouldn't cry anymore. I remembered my promise to myself as Dr. Mable handed me a napkin.

"Fuck this," I said, as I snatched the napkin out of her hand. "I told my best friend that I would come back, but never damn mind. It ain't worth it.

You ain't worth it. Where the hell you get a license from anyway?"

"Bye. Leave. I get paid for the whole hour regardless. Are you leaving or not? I got shows to catch up on."

"Really? That's all I am to you? A check?"

"I am here to help you help yourself. I'm not here to force you to be better. I have no interest in begging you to work towards healing. It does not benefit me at all to plead with you to do something for yourself. If you want to help *you,* I support it. If you don't give a damn about your mental wellness, I support you. I'm here to *help,* not beg or force. So, what's it going to be? Staying or going?"

I folded my arms and rolled my eyes. I didn't roll my eyes at her per se, but at the situation. I hated that life brought me to the point of needing therapy. It was embarrassing that I had to pay someone to help me sort out my thoughts. I was angry with myself for not choosing a conventional therapist. I wasn't sure Dr. Mable's style was for me.

She wasn't gentle. She wasn't suggestive. She was too blunt. She eased her way into nothing. She was so too the damn point! I didn't expect her to hold my hand and sing "Kumbaya," but shit. Could a bitch get some sympathy? Make me feel like I was wanted. Make me think my presence was desired. Make me believe I was important, and if I left, it would sting her a little bit. Lie to me, hell!

"*Why* are you so concerned with how I perceive you?" she asked me. "You were concerned with what I was writing. Yesterday, you wanted to know if I thought you were crazy. Now you're asking if I see you as a check. Why do you care so much about what I think about you? Why does it matter? What difference would it make? Do you worry about what other people think about you?"

I paused and thought about it. The answer was yes. "No, I don't care at all what people think about me. Doesn't make me or break me."

"Liar, Liar, pants on fire."

"You are so childish," I told her.

"But am I wrong?"

I silently said, "No."

"Please say it louder. I need you to shout to the rooftops that I was right."

I rolled my eyes at her. "Who doesn't want to be liked? Accepted? Wanted?"

"Most people do. It's human nature. But it gets dangerous when you want it from any and everybody. It gets dangerous when you start doing whatever and dealing with whatever and ignoring things just to be 'accepted'. And the truth is, after doing and dealing with and ignoring everything, you still aren't accepted by them; you're just tolerated. You're just accessible. But you're still not a necessity. You're hurting yourself."

"But it hurts so bad when people don't accept me or like me. I'm a good person. I'm kind.

I'm nice. I'm loving. I care. I'm present. Why would someone not like me? That shit hurts."

"Cry about it now so that you can heal later. Let it hurt the first time. Don't beg nobody to want or love you. Don't ask people to like you. What if I told you that people can *not* like you, and you still live?"

"I'd say that you're a got damn lie because my mom and brother have hated me my whole life, and I have felt like I was dying ever since I was old enough to understand what was going on.

"My mom hated me simply because I reminded her so much of my daddy. She never was affectionate. Never told me she loved me. Never consoled me when she saw me crying. Never asked me how my day was.

"CJ would always say things like I had funny colored eyes because I was possessed by the devil. I don't know if you can tell in this lighting, but my eyes are two different shades. They are both hazel, but one eye is a darker hazel than the other. CJ would also tell me that I was adopted, which is why I have different colored eyes than everyone else. Funny he always told me that when in the end, I found out that he was the one who possibly wasn't biologically Daddy's. I'm not sure if he is or not. That's another answer I'll never really get because everyone who I could ask is dead.

"CJ always talked about my weight. Not only was I always chubby, I was also short. So he called me Miss Piggy, no matter how many times I asked him not to.

"Daddy made it CJ's job to pick me up from the bus stop because Mama got off work late in the evening. CJ would get me from the bus stop, and he would run home, going different routes, leaving me behind and lost. Because I was chubby, I couldn't keep up with him when he would take off running, but I would try. Even though I knew how to get home from where the bus dropped me off at, I wanted to follow him. I just always wanted to be where he was. So I'd always end up lost in the neighborhood, and he never came to get me. He never looked for me. He did this from the time I was five to eight years old. It wasn't every time. But it was enough. He's six years older than me. He knew better.

"Mama knew how mean he was to me. She knew that CJ always made me cry. She knew that we never had a sibling bond. She knew there was no love from CJ towards me. And she never did anything about it. She never stepped in to try to make the relationship right."

"If your mom didn't love you, Ivory, why would she care that your brother didn't?"

Valid point.

"Even if your mom did care and intervene, she couldn't make your brother love you. But I truly believe your brother didn't love you because he didn't see the need to. He was following your mother's lead. Your mother's lack of love for you made it okay for CJ to not love you or care about you.

"But here's the thing. There's nothing you can do about that. Even if they were still alive, you couldn't do anything about that. In life, we have to learn how to know who and what we are to people and be okay with it. We have to accept that it is what it is. Peep game and let it be what it's gonna be. Cry about it, mope about it, talk shit to your best friend about it, and then let it go. Because if you don't, what happens is you become a forty-something year old adult wanting any and everybody to love you because your immediate family didn't. What happens is you start to tolerate anything just to be able to say you have people around you. What happens is you turn into… you.

"I think your father's death hurts so bad because not only was he your father, but he was the only immediate family you had that didn't make you apologize for your existence. He was the only immediate family you had that made you feel something other than regret and remorse for being born. I don't think that the pain of your father's death is from his death but from your brother's and mom's life.

"I know that on your initial paperwork you said that your main goal was to heal from your dad's death. And I want you to do that. But the only way to do that is to heal the relationship with you and your mom and brother first."

"Them bitches dead. They died before we could fix this shit!"

"They could've lived one hundred ninety-two years, and the relationship still would be a mess. Time isn't always the answer or cure. Some people just are not going to grow or change. Everybody doesn't want to be better. Some people are satisfied being the ain't shit that they are. So please stop thinking that time robbed you of healthy relationships. They were grown ass people when they died. The relationships were what they wanted them to be. Accept that. They did not want you, Ivory. The end.

"Write a letter or letters to them so that we can get to you being healed. Not only from your dad's death, but also from their existence. That's your homework. Put it all on the table in the letter or letters to them. Say everything you want to say, and hold no bars. They do not have to be alive for you to be healed from the relationships. The healing is your decision; the ball is in your court."

"I'm not a writer. At all. I'm a reader. As a matter of fact, reading has been one of my coping mechanisms. I am the founder of EyeCU Reading & Social Network book club. The members have become my sisters, and they have been my support system through all of this. They have been my family."

"That's actually awesome. It's not every day that I have a client who says they're the founder of a book club. It's not every day that I have clients who love to read, let alone be the founder of a book club! What are you reading this month?"

"This month, we're reading Complicated Simplicity by Kaylynn Hunt. Hard to put down. I already put it down to come here. And you want me to put it down to write letters?"

I laughed as if I was joking, but I was really so serious. Luna and Curtis, Jr. didn't deserve my time in no shape, form, or fashion.

"Yes, I do want you to put down that great book and write letters to your mom and brother. And the letters don't have to be perfect. They don't have to be grammatically correct. The 'i's' don't have to be dotted; the 't's' don't have to be crossed. It's to release. It's to say all the things you wish y'all would have said. It's to get it all off your chest. It's just for you.

"You're obviously not expecting an apology or changed behavior from them from the grave. You're expecting a changed behavior from *you*. This is solely about you. Think about it. Let me know if you've made a decision the next time we meet."

"Okay. Have a great day."

"You, too."

Chapter 20

I thought about that assignment all day. That assignment occupied my mind, space, thoughts, and energy. When I was supposed to be paying attention to certain things, I noticed my mind drifting. When I was supposed to be resting, I couldn't.

"Hey, Bae," Charles sang to me over dinner. "You here with me?"

"Hey, Bae," I sang back.

See. Like I said. My mind was drifting. I couldn't even spend quality time with my husband.

"I'm proud of you," he told me.

I knew he was talking about me going to therapy. It was no secret that I was hesitant in going. It also was no secret that I needed to go. I hate to admit it, but I'm glad that I went. I hate even more to admit that Dr. Mable was my therapist soulmate. She wasn't gentle at all. She was rough around the edges and straight to the point. I needed that.

"Dr. Mable has me writing a letter to Mama and CJ. She thinks that my healing starts with addressing them."

Charles looked at me confused. "Does she know that—?"

"It doesn't matter. I have to heal."

"Yes, you do, Bae. Yes, you do."

"How's the salmon?"

"I can tell you didn't cook it. Nobody makes salmon like my baby." He leaned in and pecked me on my lips. "But I don't mind eating away from home. As long as I'm with you."

"You'd say anything to get in my draws."

"You have told the truth."

He slid his hand down my inner thigh.

"Ahem." A worker cleared his throat.

"Cock blocker," Charles mumbled underneath his breath.

"That's what he gets paid to do." I grabbed his hand and kissed it.

"Dude putting in overtime."

"Don't get mad at him because the law says that you can't finger me in public."

"I'm mad that he acts like he can't mind his own damn business. I'm over here sitting on swole, and he just whistling and watching."

"I'll be sure to give it to you black licorice style when I get home. I promise."

"Oh, shit. Chit'lins making a comeback."

"Like I never left."

Charles and I hadn't had sex since Daddy went missing. There were a few failed attempts since then. Failed attempts that left me embarrassed and angry every time. Failed attempts that made me question if I was even a woman. Failed attempts that made me feel that I wasn't worthy of being anyone's girlfriend, wife, side chick—nothing. The attempts were so lackluster that I stopped trying.

Prayerfully, being healed would give us our sex life back.

Before all this, Charles and I were like rabbits. Always humping. Always kissing. Always rubbing. We had sex literally every night. It wasn't a chore. It wasn't on a calendar. It was in our loins. It was a burning urge. We had to. We were on fire every second for each other. The fact that we hadn't had sex in over a year and a half was just… pathetic. And it was all my fault.

I knew better than to withhold sex from my husband. I had had enough older women in my life to know not to do that. I always told him he could get it whenever he wanted it. But Charles was a gentleman. He didn't want to take it. He didn't want it to just be there. He wanted to caress it. He wanted it to be fed to him. He wanted it to melt in his mouth and in his hands. He wanted to be one with it. He wanted it to drip down his thighs like water springing out of a well. I couldn't provide him that, no matter how hard I tried.

But I was determined to change that.

That night, I wrote one combined letter to Luna and CJ. I didn't expect my hand to flow so freely from one side of the paper to the next. I didn't think that my thoughts would be so clear. I was shocked to know that I had so much held in.

I couldn't believe how freeing it was to write what I wrote. Even though I knew that neither one of them would ever read it or hear it, like Dr. Mable said, it was for me. I needed to write it. I needed to release it. I needed to be free of all that was weighing me down.

Chapter 21

"I wrote the letter!" I didn't even speak to Dr. Mable as I sped past her and plopped on her couch.

"I mean, hey. Did I sleep with you last night?" she asked.

"Girl, you ain't my type."

"Somebody likes it," she said, flipping her long, beautiful locs over her right shoulder.

"That somebody ain't me."

"I've been rejected by better floozies than you."

That made me laugh out loud. My grandma—my mama's mom—called everybody a floozy when she was cussing them out. To her, that was some serious cussing. Then whenever she calmed down, she would repent and put an extra five dollars in the tithing envelope at church.

"I'm sorry, Dr. Mable. Good afternoon. I'm just so excited. I got shit off my chest that I didn't even know was on there."

"Well, I'm ready whenever you are. Let me get my popcorn."

She pulled a huge tin of popcorn out of her closet. The only time I saw tins like that being sold was around Christmas. It wasn't Christmas time; it concerned me how long she had had that popcorn. But that was neither here nor there.

"My mama's name is Luna. I don't think I've ever told you that. But I wanted you to know who I am talking to in this letter."

"Okay, Ivory. Stop stalling."

"Okay." I exhaled and began to read the papers I had handwritten. "Luna, what did my daughter do to you? She is only fourteen. Just because you and I fell out doesn't mean that you had to stop having a relationship with your granddaughter. Your only granddaughter at that.

"You stopped showing up to her swim meets, Spanish quiz bowls, and school activities. You didn't even show up to Grandparents' Day or give her a Christmas gift. How fucking childish and ignorant are you?

"She went months without hearing from you. I had to force her to call you every Sunday just because I wanted her to have a better relationship with you than I had. But I heard the phone conversations. They would be so dry coming from you. She would just be talking and asking you questions, and you'd give one-word replies. I stopped forcing her to call you because I realized it was doing her more harm than good. Once she stopped calling you, that was it. She never heard your voice again.

"You knew that CJ and I hadn't spoken for over half a year, and you did nothing about it. You were aware that your only children were not talking, and you never stepped in to try to smooth it out or be the mediator or be the mender. You just love mess so damn much that you didn't care that it was coming from your children. It was your entertainment, and you loved every episode.

"I don't even know what the beef is that you had with Jackie immediately after Daddy died, but shame on you! You were so ugly towards her at the funeral. What has she ever done to you, other than take care of your two children as if we were her own? Shit. I'm lying. She treated me way better than you ever did. I guess you only acted like you liked her while Daddy was alive in hopes that he'd come back to you. Well, he didn't because he didn't want your mean, ugly-acting ass.

"Daddy didn't cheat on you with her. He didn't get her pregnant while in the middle of your divorce. He didn't even meet her until y'all had been divorced for two years. You are just mean and hateful. But even if he did cheat on you with her, so what? He's the one who was supposed to be loyal to you; she had no obligations to you.

"And where were you when I was growing up? Were you in the streets? Is that one of the problems you had with me? You couldn't be as free as you wanted to be? CJ was older, and you could go out, but you had my young ass at the house making it hard for you to break free.

"I remember wanting to go everywhere you went. If you checked the mailbox, I wanted to go. If you took the trash to the curb, I wanted to pull the can with you. You started paying me to leave you alone. I was seven years old when you paid me fifty dollars to not talk to you while you sat at the kitchen table and did… nothing. Absolutely nothing. You weren't even cooking or doing a puzzle. I was just a bother to you, and you had to get rid of me one way or the other. Well, joke's on you. I took that fifty dollars and bought a kazoo and toy drum set with it. How was that for peace?

"When I delivered Javaughn at twenty-four weeks, I was scared out of my mind. I needed the love and support of you, but you weren't supportive at all. My son was in the hospital for seven months of his precious life, and your do-nothing ass only visited him twice! ONLY TWICE did you come to see your own grandson. You had the nerve to tell me that you didn't want to see him like that, as if I did! You abandoned me and your grandson. I thought maybe, just maybe, that when you had grandchildren that it would be a second chance for you to get it right. Boy was I wrong.

"And Curtis, Jr. Because of you, I know what a backhanded compliment is. You could never say, 'Ivory, that's a pretty color on you.' It'd always be, 'Ivory, that's a pretty color on you. That black makes you look less stubby and short.' Instead of saying, 'Your house looks nice,' you'd say, 'Your house looks better than that old slump you moved out of.'

"Maybe you had to do that to make yourself feel better. Maybe my presence and existence were so intimidating to you that you had to do or say *something* to alleviate your discomfort. But I honestly thank you for that. Because I always sought your approval that I would never receive, that became my fuel to always go bigger to be better.

"Our disconnect is because of you. I don't know what I did or didn't do to you, but I genuinely am sorry. But if there is something that I did or didn't do, you were never man enough to tell me what it is. Whatever my offense was, that could have been a conversation between us. But instead of talking to me, you allowed the disconnect and separation to span for our entire lives. That disconnection and separation extended to our children. Our children are first cousins and have no relationship with each other.

"And, CJ, I'll never forget how you showed your ass shortly after Javaughn passed. Telling me things like I needed to get over him and that I should get rid of his things. You were insensitive and flat-out rude. Not brotherly or loving at all. Yet, you claimed to be a man of God. You had no idea of the inner turmoil that I was battling. I was sad, depressed, and a shell of my former self. In hindsight, I realize that you felt like Javaughn needing so much attention was taking away from our mother's and father's attention for your son. You had just adopted him, and you didn't feel he was getting the love and attention he deserved because of Javaughn. Everything with you was a one-sided competition.

"Most times I would ignore your ignorance, foolishness, and your insensitivities, but when you told me that I should clean out his room and get rid of his things was when I snapped!

" 'Why do you have to be such a bitch?!' I hollered at you. You weren't ready for my snapback. You were so used to sweet, quiet, passive Ivory. But not that day. You had gone too far. You were so stunned that I spoke up for myself that you decided you were gonna go home because I needed 'time to cool down.' You thought we were gonna sweep it under the rug like we always did. That argument resulted in a two-year hiatus of us not talking until you found out I was pregnant with Mychaela.

"That day of our blow up was the day that I decided I was done being your puppy. No more following you around and begging for your attention. You could go to hell for all I care. And by the looks of your pathetic life, you were already in hell.

"CJ, you even took me and our two sisters to court over Daddy's assets. You won his houses. You even sued Jackie for half his assets. She had been taking care of Daddy for the last twenty-five years of his life. Daddy owed her everything. A lot more than what he left her. But you still took half of the *nothing* that he left her. I'm not even mad about you taking my inheritance from me. I'm mad that when the courts gave you my and our sisters' inheritances, you didn't share them with Jackie.

You surely could have shared it with the woman who kept his health in order. But you were too greedy and evil to do that.

"Ever since we were kids, I took the brunt of your disrespect and turned the other cheek. After all the put-downs I endured from you, all I ever tried to do was be a good sister to you. Yet, you remained a hateful, disrespectful, spiteful, jealous, self-centered asshole to me! No matter what I did, you always gave me your ass to kiss.

"And I could go on and on with you two. But I'll stop there. You both know what you did to me. You both know what you didn't do for me. You both know what you made me endure.

"But I forgive you. Both of you. You no longer possess the power to control me. I no longer seek your approval. I need not a damn thing else from you. I am no longer bamboozled into thinking that I need either one of you to survive.

"I have no idea where you guys are. I don't know where you are working, if you're working at all. I don't know if either one of you have moved. I don't know how to find you. I don't even want to know. It doesn't matter at all. Because even though I have forgiven the both of you and wish you both nothing but the best, you two are **dead to me.**"

I proudly put the letter down with a smile on my face. The weight was lifted off of me. I could finally smile again. My peace was being restored. I could notice the sunlight beaming through Dr.

Mable's window. I hadn't noticed the sunlight since the day I found out my dad was missing.

Dr. Mable stared at me. She never blinked. I knew what she was going to say. I knew what she was going to say when I was writing the letter. But I didn't care. She said I needed to be healed, so that's what I did: I did what I had to do and wrote what I had to write and said what I had to say to be healed.

"Your mother and brother aren't dead? They aren't in a grave? They aren't in a mausoleum? They aren't cremated? Their bodies aren't products of science?" Dr. Mable asked me.

"Not to my knowledge," I answered.

"To your knowledge, your brother and mom are alive?"

"Yes. To my knowledge."

"I'll be damned," she whispered.

"I never meant to deceive you or lie to you. They really are dead… to me."

"Ivory, I get it. I really do. I understand that. I have three ex-husbands who are dead to me. I have a raping uncle who is dead to me. I have a son who is dead to me.

"My problem with this situation is I didn't hear you say that you tried to mend these relationships. Did you ever call them out on their shit? Did you ever pick up the phone and say, 'I feel this way. Let's talk about it.'? Because if you haven't told people their offenses, you can't hold the offenses against them.

"So, my question is, have you been woman enough or Christian enough to go to them and tell them how you feel?"

"What does being a Christian have to do with anything?"

"Because Matthew 18:15 says that if your brother offends you, tell him."

"My brother didn't offend me by himself. My mother offended me, too."

"Look, Smart Ass, you know good and damn well that scripture covers every gender and every relationship. You gonna put your big girl draws on or not?"

I exhaled. "They know what they did. They know that they ain't shit."

"We can't assume that shit knows it stinks. Somebody gotta tell him. Or *her*, Smart Ass."

"I haven't said those words to them, no. But they know that I'm mad. They know that we haven't spoken in over a year. It hasn't bothered them. Why should it bother me?"

"But it obviously bothers you. You writing four-page letters like you're Aaliyah and shit. You don't write all them pages if you're unbothered."

"I'll think about it. That's all I can promise you. I will think about it."

"That's all I can ask. As far as the letter, I usually have my patients to tie them to a balloon and set it free. But maybe you should read it to them if you decide to contact them. You are more than welcome to bring them here, no extra charge. I definitely suggest that you amend the letter though. Soften it up. You can catch more flies with honey. Make the letter a little more gentle."

"*That,* I won't do. They gonna get it in its rawest form."

"More flies with honey."

"Fuck that."

"Okay. I'll definitely be seeing you for more years then. Because reading that letter as-is will cause more problems, and your relationship will get worse."

"I've gone my whole life without them. Believe me. I'll be fine."

"Okay. It is solely your choice. I am so proud of you for writing that letter. How do you feel after writing it?"

"Like the elephant has been removed off my chest. I can start getting back to me."

"That is great. This is progress. See you next week?"

"Most definitely."

Chapter 22

But I didn't feel like an elephant had been lifted off my chest. I felt like two more had been added. Dr. Mable was right. I had not done all that I could do to mend fences. I wasn't going to be able to really rest until I did.

September 30, 2020, was the last time my mom and I spoke to each other. It was on the phone, and I still remember our last conversation quite vividly.

She wasn't much of a talker without you having to draw conversation out of her. Our conversations always felt one-sided. I'd fish for questions to keep the conversation flowing while she'd answer with short responses.

On this particular day, same as always, the conversation started with our normal pleasantries. We'd talked about the weather, what we were watching on TV, and what we were having for dinner. I was making salmon croquettes, yellow rice, and green beans while she was ranting and raving about the Trader Joe's mandarin orange chicken that I'd left in her driveway due to the pandemic's social distancing requirement. She kept talking about how good and juicy it was with "just the right amount of sweet."

I had something I dreaded asking her, but I needed to just put on my big girl panties and let it rip. Nobody likes talking about death, but my father had left his affairs in such a mess that I needed to ask my mother what her final wishes were. CJ and I weren't on speaking terms, so I figured I'd better find out for myself so that if anything were to happen, we could come together and honor her final wishes like civil adults. After everything that I thought I knew as the truth turning out to be a lie, if life had taught me anything, it was that my family couldn't be trusted, so I needed to get answers directly from the horse's mouth.

Those days, all my mother and I ever talked about was how this monstrous coronavirus didn't discriminate. The world was originally informed that it mostly affected the elderly, but we were now starting to see it spread viciously throughout all ages. I eased my way into the topic by telling my mother about my thirty-two-year-old Facebook friend, wife, and mother of 3 whose life had sadly been claimed by the virus. I then said, "None of us are promised tomorrow."

She responded with, "You got that right!"

I continued with, "You know with how my father left things in such a mess, CJ and I not being on speaking terms, and me not knowing if we'll ever be on speaking terms, I really would like to hear from you directly on what your wishes are."

Man, did this strike a chord! She went off! "What do you mean? My wishes?! Cremate me, and I ain't leaving y'all shit! I ain't got a dime to leave to y'all! There's enough money to bury me, and this house is going back to the bank! I've prayed for you and CJ, and y'all need to get your shit together!"

"Ma, I think you misunderstood me. I don't expect anything from you. I'm not asking you what you're leaving us. I'm saying with the way people are falling like flies and how my father left his affairs in such a mess, I just simply wanted to ask for myself what your wishes are. What would happen if you got sick? What would happen if you needed to be resuscitated? What kind of service do you wish to have, insurance coverage, burial stuff?"

She screamed, "I DON'T GIVE A FUCK! I'll be dead! Curtis, Jr. knows what I want! I've prayed for you and CJ for years, and y'all need to get your shit together. CJ told me y'all ain't talking because of that bitch Jackie. She said y'all haven't spoken since the funeral."

I was stunned with a double whammy. I wasn't even aware that she knew that CJ and I weren't speaking. And what was her issue with Jackie for her to call her a bitch?

"Wow! Well, you're the mother. You mean to tell me that you've known all along that CJ and I haven't spoken since the funeral, and you said nothing? And what's going on with you and Jackie for you to call her a bitch? Shame on you! CJ is lying. It has nothing at all to do with Jackie."

She screamed into the phone, "Shame on yo' own damn self! Humph! Yeah, I'm the mother, but you and CJ are grown! All we have left are each other, and all I can do is pray for y'all to get your shit together. And fuck Jackie! I should've punched that bitch in her motherfucking face when I saw her the other day. You didn't tell me she was gonna be at your house when you invited me over!"

Again, I was stunned because as far as I'd known, she's never had a problem with Jackie. For years, my mother had gone to family dinners at my father's and Jackie's house, and there'd never been a problem.

"I ain't gotta tell you shit! She's a bitch, and the next time I see her, I'm punching her in her motherfucking face!" she screamed.

That's when I realized that the problem that she had with Jackie was that somehow it got back to her that Jackie's friend Ms. Victoria told me that Daddy was not CJ's real dad. When her friend told me that, Jackie was there, and she had not confirmed or denied what the friend said. But if Luna would have just calmed down, been an adult, and stated the problem, I could have told her that CJ was the first one to tell me that Daddy was not his daddy. All Jackie's friend did was validate what CJ told me. Both times that I was told that, it had nothing to do with Jackie. Luna was mad at the wrong person. And the friend who told me was a mutual friend of hers and Jackie. She really should have been upset with her friend Ms. Victoria if anybody.

Yes, CJ is a liar. But I'm not convinced that CJ told Luna that we weren't speaking because of Jackie. I believe Luna needed an excuse to have a problem with Jackie because she really didn't have a valid reason to be at odds with her.

The "secret" that my father was not CJ's biological father was one secret that Luna planned to take to the grave.

During this last conversation between Luna and me, Luna started talking about how she, CJ, and I needed to go to therapy, but retracted the suggestion as soon as it left her lips by calmly saying, "I ain't going nowhere in the middle of a pandemic."

Going from one extreme to the next, she was coming unraveled unlike I'd ever seen her. She'd gone from bashing my love for books to my church home to my husband's role in the church. After accepting we weren't going to get anywhere, I calmly said, "I'm gonna let you go now."

Without waiting for a response, I ended the call, and that was the last time that I spoke to my mother.

Chapter 23

"My therapist had the nerve to suggest that I reach out to CJ and Luna," I told Charles. "As if I owe them something."

"You don't. But you owe you something."

"What you mean?"

"Ivory, you miss them, and you miss you. If you want nothing else, you want closure."

He was right. Ugh, I hated when he was right. He started to do a dance, and a grin ran across his face.

"What?" I rolled my eyes. I knew what.

He sang, "I'm right, and you know it."

"As long as you know."

"Oh, no, Ma'am. You gotsta say it."

"My throat is getting so dry. I can't speak all of a sudden."

"Oh, but you can say that."

We both laughed, wrapped in each other's arms.

"Reach out to them. And be honest. Even tell them that you have been in this mental facility for a little over a month. Let them know that you've been seeing Dr. Mable here, and she thinks that family counseling is a good idea."

"That's the part that I don't want to reveal. That I'm locked up in a white coat in an insane asylum. That's another one-up CJ will have over me. That I lost my damn mind."

"Quit being so damn dramatic, Ivory. You are not locked up. You roam freely inside and outside. You can have a cell phone. You DoorDash salmon all the damn time. You are not in a white coat. You are in a purple romper with Balenciagas on your feet. Every day, you get to eat breakfast, lunch, and dinner with Que or me or both. And you voluntarily admitted yourself here. You were not hauled off in a van after being accosted.

"Your dad died, Ivory. You became depressed because of that. You sought help. The end. And CJ could never one-up you. You are married to me. It don't get no better than this. I *am* the prize, dammit!"

"The prize that never shuts the hell up."

"Then put something in my mouth and make me."

My cheeks instantly turned red. It didn't take much for my yellow ass to blush.

"Charles," I whispered, "we'll get caught."

"I don't care."

I looked around the dining room. Not one person was paying us attention. But dinner just started. If we got up to leave and went to my room, everyone would know why.

"I tell you what." I rubbed his hand. "When I come home, I'll put whatever you want me to in your mouth."

"You better." He winked at me. "You going to call them?" he asked me.

"I don't have their numbers, and I unsaved them as contacts in my phone."

"Don't even try it. I have their numbers," Charles said to me.

"Well, I don't want to talk to them. I'd rather send them a message. I'll unblock them on Facebook and start there."

"I can be there for you while you do that," he offered.

I took him up on it. We went to my room. I lied on his chest, went to Facebook, and unblocked CJ. I scrolled down his wall and was taken back by what I saw. "Free Curtis, Jr." was all on his wall by different people.

"He's in jail?" Charles asked, in shock.

He couldn't have been more shocked than me. The more I scrolled, the more it became real to me. Then I got to one post that posted a link to his arrest.

Fifty-four-year-old Curtis Jones, Jr. was the driver when his car crossed the median on I-75, side-swiping an 18-wheeler... The passenger in his car, seventy-three-year-old Luna Hopkins, is listed in critical condition... Jones had minor injuries and was arrested at the scene for drunk driving... The driver of the 18-wheeler died at the scene... No bail has been set for Jones... This is his sixth DUI... Stay tuned as we follow this story.

"Oh, my God." I exhaled the words. "Oh, my God."

"That was a month ago. Your mom was in the car with him. I wonder if your mom…"

"I am terrified to unblock her and see."

"I'll do it." Charles took my phone, unblocked Luna, and scrolled her page. "A lot of pictures of her in recovery. She's still alive. This pic of her feeding herself was posted earlier this morning."

For a second, I was relieved at the thought of her being dead. It meant I could fully let her go. But she was alive. That meant I had to try to make it right with her.

Sigh.

"I'm going to call her stepsister and get the details," I told Charles.

My mom had no living siblings. She had two stepsisters and two stepbrothers. I had no relationship with any of them. Luna did, though, so I assumed they knew *something*.

Aunt Toni answered the phone really dry-like. That was her personality, so I tried to not take it personally. It didn't matter anyway. She told me what I wanted to know.

She told me that it was touch and go for Luna for a minute, and it didn't look like she was going to make it, but she made it. Aunt Toni told me that Luna had to have brain surgery, a hip replacement, shoulder surgery, and she lost an eye. She said that Luna was looking at, at least three more weeks in the hospital and a minimum of six weeks rehabilitation after the hospital. I asked how

Luna is mentally, and her answer was, "She's still Luna."

Damn. That brain injury didn't make her a decent human being?

Aunt Toni told me the hospital and room number Luna was at. Charles told me that whenever I was released from the hospital, we'd go see her wherever she was. I looked forward to it, and I feared it.

I feared how she would look. Missing an eye? All these surgeries? What lingering effects was she dealing with? Could she walk? Walk normally? Talk? Talk normally? Did she have a limp? A slur?

I also feared what I would say. Would I comment on her appearance? Should I act like I didn't notice? Should I take it easy on her since she was recovering?

I feared what she would say. Did this wreck make her even more bitter? Or worse. Did it make her reachable and accessible to where she'd listen to my concerns and try to be a better mom? I honestly didn't know how to handle having a relationship with her. I got accustomed to not having her. What if she actually wanted to be in my life?

I stopped Dr. Mable in the hallway and told her that I took her up on her suggestion of bringing them to therapy, but they literally couldn't come. She asked me if I was serious about seeing them. I told her I was. Her words to me were, "Then I'll make it happen."

The next day, she told me that the facility van would take me to see my mom later that day and that she set up a visitation with the prison for me to see CJ the next day. Due to technicalities, Dr. Mable couldn't come with me to either one. No one could come with me, actually. I had to face the beasts alone.

I talked to my daughter on the phone every night before going to bed. I told her every night that I was away getting help at the facility so that I could be better whenever I came back. I had too many years left of being a mother. I didn't take that responsibility lightly.

I explained to her that therapy was helping me be better to myself so that I could be better to her. It was hard being a mother when my heart was breaking. It was hard to be present in all ways in her life when my mind was betraying me. I put an end to the devil stealing me from my daughter. She deserved all of me, and I was making sure that she got what she deserved.

Mychaela was so understanding and patient. She couldn't visit me because she was under eighteen, but we Facetimed every day. She told me she was proud of me and to take however long I needed. God surely remembered me when it was time to give me a wonderful daughter. I could not have prayed to receive anyone better.

Chapter 24

I've always hated hospitals ever since my son died in the hospital at eleven months old. Ever since his death, I associated hospitals with being a dream snatcher and a place where faith goes to die. I believed that so much that I gave birth to my daughter at home. A hospital was not a place for hope. So, being in that hospital, walking to my mom's room with all kinds of uncertainties, made a feeling I can't explain wash over me.

I wanted someone to hold my hand so bad. Charles, Que, Dr. Mable, even Mychaela. Somebody. But I had to wear my big girl draws and do it alone.

That walk to her room was the longest, loneliest stroll I'd ever experienced. The twists and turns of the hall didn't make it any better. And being stopped to be told to make sure I keep my mask on didn't make it any better. COVID and anxiety weren't the best combination.

I looked at her room number on the door: **2**. I was there. That was the destination. Two. Two chances to get my family back. First was with Luna; the second was with Curtis, Jr.

Sigh. *Here it goes.*

I knocked on the closed door with the letter I had written to her and CJ in my hand. I waited on an answer, but I never got one. I didn't know if she was asleep or if she was able to talk, so I just walked in.

Her eyes met mine. It felt like being reunited with an ex. The awkwardness, excitement, uncertainty, anger, happiness—all of it.

"Hi."

I'm not sure which one of us said it. I'm not sure which one of us spoke back.

"How are you? How you feeling?" I asked.

"I've been praying that you'd come. I don't know how you found out. I just know that prayer works."

My mommy prayed to see me. I felt like a little kid in the candy store. I was squeaking like a mouse on the inside and grinning like a Cheshire cat on the outside.

I quickly and discreetly folded the letter and placed it in my purse. *More flies with honey,* I thought to myself.

"Well, my mental health has been taking hits ever since I found out Daddy was missing. It finally got the best of me, and I admitted myself into a mental health facility. I'm in therapy. My therapist felt that it would be conducive to my healing if I mend things with you."

"Do you feel that way? Or are you here because of a doctor's order?"

"My heart brought me here," I admitted.

Her face was slightly crooked, and her speech was slightly slurred, but not to the point of not being understandable. Or maybe because I talked to Daddy for over twenty years after he had a stroke that left him speech impaired, I felt that her speech was understandable. There was a patch over her right eye. I watched her keep her right arm guarded and on her abdomen. When she would shift her body weight, her right side didn't move as quickly or fluidly as her left side. I'm not sure that I saw her right leg move at all.

"Yeah. That drinking and drugging finally got the best of CJ," she said, after watching me watch her body movements. "I guess I'm crazy for getting in the car with his drunk-high ass. I knew he had had too many and too much. But I have such bad night vision that I took my chances. Shit. Looking back, my driving couldn't have left me worse than this."

"Why had he been drinking and doing drugs?"

"Because he's Curtis, Jr. He's a damn feening drunk. We were just out doing regular stuff: grocery store run, window shopping at the mall, dinner at a restaurant. I noticed he kept swallowing pills and drinking out this Tumbler. I assumed it was water and Tylenol, but as the day went on, his speech kept getting worse, and he started getting mad at nothing. Then he ordered a margarita at the restaurant. That… whew."

"And y'all were on the way home?"

"To my house, yes. I don't know what made him swerve over the median. I ask him all the time. He can't give me an answer."

"You remember?"

"I remember everything. I had brain surgery because of fluid on my brain from a blunt head injury. But I don't have no amnesia or nothing like that. I'm all the way here!"

"That's good. That's really good."

At some point I had sat down on the couch. Conversation was flowing. I was at ease. I had been anxious for nothing.

"I got a long road ahead of me. Physical therapy, occupational therapy, speech therapy, mental therapy. Therapy, therapy, therapy. Ugh."

"The alternative is death."

"The alternative is me never getting my black ass in that car in the first place."

"I understand that."

"Whatever brought you here, thank you."

"Well, I want to talk about how you've made me feel my whole life. Like I was a burden. Like I was bothering you. Like you regretted me."

"Well, you weren't any of those things," she dryly said.

"What was I to you?"

"My daughter! What do you mean?"

"Was I the apple of your eye? Did you think about me when you were away at work? Were you reminded of me whenever you saw black because that's my favorite color? Did you know that was my favorite color? Did I ever cross your mind?"

"What kind of questions are these? Aren't you my daughter? Don't you have a daughter? Girl, don't start this."

"Can you answer the question? You always treated CJ better than me. I just want answers. I'm tired of feeling like this."

"I'm not answering nothing. You came up here to start mess. Don't you think I've been through enough?"

I wasn't going to back down.

"Why you stopped checking on Mychaela? Your only granddaughter. What did she do to you?"

"It was obvious you had a problem with me. I thought it would be disrespectful to keep talking to her."

"It had nothing to do with her."

"Now I know you don't mind me talking to her."

"You could have asked me. You just went on with life like she doesn't exist."

"Well, I would hope that you told her that's not true."

"I can tell her whatever I want. She goes by your actions. And I tried my best to keep her out of grown folks' business. I wasn't going to involve her in our mess until you started treating her differently."

"I'm sorry, Mychaela."

"She's not here to hear you."

"I will call her. Same number?"

"Yes," I answered her. "And CJ lies so much. He's the one who said that Daddy is not his real dad. Jackie has never confirmed it or denied it, but is that true? Is Jackie waiting on the real answer like I am? Is Daddy Curtis, Jr.'s daddy or not?"

"Did your therapist tell you to come here and start shit with me?!"

"She told me to come and get healed."

"If your healing means fucking with me, you're going to die wounded. Goodbye, Ivory. I thought we were getting somewhere. I thought you seeing me like this would change something. But you're the same ole whiny, annoying, complaining little runt. Girl. Good. Bye."

Dr. Mable told me to accept people as they are. Expect that person from that person. Not to be surprised when people act like themselves. I took that nugget and put it in my pocket. I walked out of her hospital room with my head held high knowing that I tried. That's all I could do, and I did it.

Chapter 25

Dr. Mable came and sat on my bed that night. She was working late when she saw my door open.

"I don't get in people's bed for free," she said.

"My insurance is paying you to do whatever I want you to do."

We laughed together.

"I'm on my way home. Just peeped in and saw you. Your face says it all. I can read your body and tell you didn't get the results you wanted. But you tried. You can scratch trying off the list."

"I hate that it was ever on the list in the first place. I knew what to expect."

"Then you shouldn't be hurt. And believe me, if you didn't try, in the future, you would have been on my couch saying, 'I should have tried. I could've reached out. I needed to do this and do that. Blah, blah, blah. Waah, waah, waah.' "

"It wouldn't have been today, though. That's a fact."

"But we're forward thinkers. We look down the street and prepare for the wreck that's in three miles. You did good. And you know you did."

"Sure."

"The goal wasn't for her to be different when you left. It was for *you* to be different when you left. Now you know what to expect. You know where you stand. No gray areas. And the same goes for when you go see your brother tomorrow. *You* will leave a different person. *You* are the one who is willing to change. This meeting is just to tie up loose ends and to color in the gray areas. Dassit! Dassall! Healing is your responsibility, and it's in *your* hands. Nobody is responsible for how you feel and heal but you. Capisce?"

"Capisce."

We fist bumped.

"See you tomorrow on my way to the time clock. But don't talk to me before I've had my orange juice," Dr. Mable said.

"That's how I am about my banana and turkey bacon. Don't even wave at me until I've had my banana and turkey bacon."

Dr. Mable looked me in my face and said, "I'll eat turkey bacon when I see a turkey pig."

This woman was as crazy as a fish with titties. And I loved her with everything in me. She was who I needed. She was my saving grace. I'm so glad I chose her out of the other therapists in the facility.

"Good night, Ivory." She smiled at me.

"Good night."

****

Who the hell is the prisoner? Them or me? I thought to myself as I was going through the process to visit CJ with all the clank clanks I heard from the gates slamming behind me. One gate not opening until the last one closed. Then the COVID screens. My God. Did they want my mother's maiden name and the name of my first pet, too? Shit.

I had to leave my cell phone and the letter that I had written to him in the car. They patted me down for weapons. That was some bullshit because the damn inmates have phones and weapons, but the visitors can't. Visitors ain't the threat; the inmates are.

When I sat at the table to wait on him, it hit me that I was visiting my brother in prison. *Prison.* My brother was a prisoner, an inmate, a convict... a murderer.

My nerves had time to show their ass. The more I sat and waited, the more my mind wandered. The more the scenarios were created in my mind. The more the possible outcomes were changing.

"Long time no see," CJ said, as he plopped down in the chair.

I was a hugger. Even when I didn't like the person, I wanted to hug. But I kept my hands to myself. I'm not sure that was allowed in the prison anyway. They made me sign so many papers of what I wasn't allowed to do, it would've been smart of me to just ask them what I could do.

"Ditto," I said.

"What you want?"

He smelled like alcohol. All the things that they pat us down for before entering prison, but my brother, the inmate, could be intoxicated.

"Closure. A better relationship. Answers. Something," I replied to his question.

"What?" His face scrunched up.

"Ever since we were kids—"

"Ivory! You damn near one hundred years old, and you want to talk about when we were kids?"

"I don't want to talk about when we were kids. I want to talk about our relationship, why it's like it is, what we can do to change it."

"It is what it is because you are spoiled and entitled. It is what it is because you want the world to kiss your ass. I ain't the one."

"You have been ugly towards me ever since we were kids. You made fun of me, mistreated me—"

"Oh, my God, Ivory. If you had friends, you would know from them that that is normal sibling rivalry. You should have made fun of me back, mistreated me back. You are complaining that I was a brother to you."

"I don't express love through abuse."

"Well, good for you, Michelle Obama. Let me guess, when people go low, you go high?"

"Yes. I do. I know how to joke with someone and take a joke, but you were outright cruel. And let me guess. Taking Daddy's assets and cheating me out of my inheritance was just part of sibling rivalry?"

"There was money to be had. Not my fault you didn't get it. You gotta be quicker than that."

"Daddy worked so hard for everything he had. You didn't deserve any of it, CJ."

"Your daddy was a lot of things, but a hard worker wasn't one of them. He owed me."

"Why you all of a sudden so angry at him and calling him *my* daddy? Y'all were so close. What happened?"

"Things I'll never talk about. But in the end, he made it clear that he wasn't my dad. He made it clear that he was your dad and your dad only."

CJ would lie about what color shirt he was wearing. I wasn't believing that. He and Daddy ate dinner and went to church together every week up until he went missing. Daddy did nothing to him, and he knew that. He was just greedy. He loved material possessions more than he loved Daddy.

"Was he your real dad?"

"No, Ivory! Accept that! How many times you want me to tell you that? How many times you gonna ask me that? I've told you, Ms. Victoria told you, Jackie never denied it. What more do you want?! Do I even look like him at all?!

"Mama and Curtis told me that when I was in elementary school. You are nobody for me to lie to. You are not that damn special. Shit! You were special to Mama and Curtis. That's why they lied to you. I don't love you enough to lie to you. I damn sure don't like you enough to lie to you."

"Why not? Why don't you love me? Why don't you like me?"

"Why don't you love me? Why don't you like me?" he mocked me, in a falsetto tone.

"I just want a better life, CJ. I want a brother. I want a relationship with you. I am heavy with grief and sorrow. Depression is eating me alive. I can't leave here with our relationship being the same as when I came here. I am in therapy. I am living in a mental facility. That's how bad my life is, CJ."

"Seriously?! You show up to visit me in prison with a Louis Vuitton hair clip in your hair and one thousand dollar diamonds in your ears, and you have the nerve to tell me how bad you have it? Bitch, I'm behind bars all day, and when I'm not, I'm in handcuffs. But *your* life is so bad? *I'm* the one living the dream? Fuck outta here.

"You want to talk about the half a million dollars I won and the houses and land? None of that shit means anything in here. I can use none of it! I'm already serving six years for violating my probation. They haven't even set my court date for my other charges, but I'm looking at fifty-five years minimum. Life, max. In both cases, no possibility of parole. I'm being charged with DUI, reckless endangerment, and manslaughter. No bail set. I have to sit here and rot. Daddy died for nothing."

"Did you kill Daddy for the money?"

He leaned in to me and intertwined all ten of his fingers. "Ivory Marie Stevans, are you stupid?"

"No, I'm not!"

"Do you have trouble piecing together clues?" he asked me.

"No."

"You comprehend things pretty well?"

"Yes," I confidently answered.

"Then I don't have to answer that question. You know everything you need to know." He stood up and began walking towards the door. He looked back at me and said, "Don't come back here. I'm taking you off of my visitors' list. You and your Louis Vuitton have a great day."

I grabbed his hand, stopping him from walking. "What did you and Sandra Barker talk about that day on the phone when we were looking for Daddy? When the only person she would talk to was you?"

CJ leaned down and whispered in my ear, "That I would share with her whatever I won if and when Daddy came up dead."

"And what were you and Daddy arguing about at Bangy's?"

He pulled himself out of my grasp, slyly grinned at me, walked away, and never looked back.

"You bitch! You fucking useless piece of space! I hate you! You crusty, drunk ho'!" I yelled at him from my table to the door he was walking towards. My hands hurt from slapping the table over and over so forcefully.

Right before he walked through the exit door, I reached for a chair to throw at him, but I heard my dad's voice in my head, "I'm going to haunt him for the rest of his life. Leave before they make you somebody's cellmate."

"I'm fine! I'm done. I quit," I said to the guard walking towards me. "I will see my way out."

I cried in the van all the way back to the mental health facility. I cried because he gave me no closure. I cried because he wouldn't bend. I cried because he admitted to killing my daddy without admitting it. *My* daddy. I couldn't protect him the way he protected me. I failed him. I failed myself. I failed life.

The worse thing is that I still couldn't prove he killed him. He would deny it to his grave. He obviously did a good job with his murder because the case was cold and closed. And he did it for nothing. He couldn't even enjoy his assets that he won-slash-stole, and his selfish ass still wouldn't share it with Jackie.

Fuck Curtis, Jr. Fuck Luna. I took the letter that I wrote to CJ and Luna, ripped it to shreds, put it in the toilet, shit on it, and flushed it. To hell with the both of them.

Chapter 26

"But CJ did give you closure. The closure is that there will never be closure. You know that now. You can move on. Begin the next chapter. Cry and move on. Be pissed and move on. Be mad and move on," Dr. Mable said.

"I'm so mad at my daddy, and I'm so apologetic to him. He left everything a mess. All these women he was in and out with. Didn't have a true will. Didn't leave a beneficiary. Just had money and assets everywhere, out in the open for the taking. And CJ took it. I didn't protect him. He could still be here."

"Ivory, I thank you for your cooperation every step of the way. Whether you wanted to do it or not, you did everything I asked and suggested. The nurses say that you're taking your meds. The counselor says that you participate in group and the group activities. Thank you so much for doing this for you.

"What I'm going to ask you to do next is the most important part of your progress. If you do nothing else, I need you to do this."

My throat dropped into my chest. What the hell was she going to ask me to do? Beg Luna and CJ for forgiveness when I did nothing wrong? Eat meat with bones in it? Work on a Sunday? What?

"Okay," I said, hesitantly.

"Write your dad a letter."

"Huh?"

"Write him a letter."

"And say what?"

"Whatever you want to. What you wish you would have said. What you wish you could have said. Any random things that you wanted to say. Just… let your heart write the letter. And you don't have to read it to me. But you must do this for you."

She put a balloon and string in my hand and sent me on my way.

I had so much anger towards my daddy that I was more excited to write the letter to him than I was to Luna and CJ. Between him possibly lying to me my whole life about being CJ's dad, him not making Mama be a better mama to me, him whoring and having children all across Detroit who I was deprived of growing up with, leaving shit a mess in his death, I was fed up with him.

Crazy that in the midst of all that anger, my letter to him started off with, "I'm sorry".

I'm sorry for not protecting you. I'm sorry for not letting you know of every time you offended me because that deprived you of the chance to make it right. I'm sorry for not showing up and saving you.

I'm sorry for not visiting you more. We should have gone to church together more. We should have had more lunches and dinners together. I should have randomly popped up at your door more just to say, 'Look at my new socks'. I should have called you more on lunch breaks. I just thought we had more time.

Not a day goes by that I don't think of you, and whenever I close my eyes, you're with me. I think about the way your big presence could shift the dynamic of the room. When you walked into a room, you could either light it up or make it go dim, depending on your mood.

I think about the way you loved and supported your grandkids. You were always there for every milestone and every event. All I had to do was tell you the date once, and you were there. I think about your sneaky smile, mannish jokes, and gut-busting laughter. Man, you had no filter. None!

I used to laugh at how you always left voicemails that said, "Ivory, it's your father," as if I didn't know your voice. But you always ended each message by saying, "I love you." You know, when you died, I kept lots of your voicemails so that when I get in my feelings, I can listen to you say, "I love you" one more time. And all of the pictures and selfies we took, I look at them often.

You know, after you died and some truths came to light, I was mad at you. I was big mad at you! You always taught me to have my house in order, but you left yours in such a mess. Never did I imagine that you were the glue that bonded me, my mother, and CJ together. The day you died, everything went to shit.

You could've told me, Daddy! You could've told me that Curtis, Jr. wasn't your biological child.

It didn't change the fact that he was still my brother, but it sure explained a hell of a lot! It wouldn't have changed my love for him.

From where I stood, you never treated him any different than you treated me. You showed us both love. What one of us got, the other got. Why keep it from me?! What were you thinking?! How is it that everybody knew but me?! I wish I could talk to you one more time to get closure.

When I think back, I was just a little girl looking for her big brother's love, acceptance, and approval, but he always treated me like I was gum stuck on the bottom of his shoe. Things make so much more sense now, but it didn't have to be that way if the parents that we trusted were just honest with us… me.

Now that I know what I know, your and my conversations take on a whole new meaning. In hindsight, I think you were always telling me bits and pieces about not being his dad without telling me the whole truth. But now I'm left feeling like my whole life has been a lie, so I'm in therapy, and I have a lot of talks with God. I talk out loud to you, too, so I hope you can hear me.

Thinking that you married our mother, knowing she was pregnant with another man's child, yet still accepting, loving, giving him your full name, and raising CJ as your own was very noble of you. Holding on to that thought has helped me let go of some of the anger and open my heart to forgiveness. I believe that your intentions were good, but ultimately, they did more harm than good.

I'm still working on forgiving my mother.

Thank God memories exist out of time. I love and miss you so much, Daddy. I know that as long as I live, you'll be with me forever. I feel your presence often, and I know you're watching over me. I dream that one day I'll see you in heaven where I'll be able to hug your neck and sit on your lap like a big baby and take some more selfies.

Until then, rest well, Daddy. You'll never be dead to me. You'll forever live on in my heart. It's gonna be lights, camera, and action when EyeCU again.

I forgive you for not coming back for me. I forgive you for all the lies. I forgive you for not telling me that you weren't CJ's real dad. I forgive you for leaving the mess behind. I forgive you for breaking my heart.

I forgive you.

I folded the letter, blew up the balloon that Dr. Mable gave me, and tied the letter to the balloon. I walked outside to the balcony. The view overlooked a pond that was full of fish. I thought about Daddy. He loved fishing. Growing up, he always told me that catfish have periods. I never researched or Googled that to find out. I'll let that be one of the things that I hold on to in remembrance of him.

I let the balloon go.

Chapter 27

I woke up to a missed call and voicemail from Luna. "If you want to talk, come back," is what the voicemail she left said.

The facility cleared me to go back to the hospital since it was considered a part of my treatment. They drove me there and waited on me outside.

I walked in her room. Before I could speak or sit down, she began talking.

"I treated CJ better because of the guilt that I carried around for Curtis not being his biological dad. I'm not even able to give him his biological dad because I don't know who he is."

"My God. Were you raped?"

"Ha! I wish. I was just enjoying my life. 'Doing me' as you young kids say. I didn't know any of those men. Some, I met in clubs. Some, I worked with. Some, hell, they were just there. I gave six men a DNA test—the six that I could recall. Of course, as luck would have it, none of them were his dad.

"You had a dad. I did right by you. I owed him so much. Not giving a child a dad is just torture. I was always overdoing and overachieving with him so that he wouldn't feel left out.

"And when I found out he was gay, I felt like it was my fault and that I owed him something extra. I knew that he had a lifetime of hell and hatred ahead of him because of who he was attracted to. Maybe if he had his own daddy in his life, he wouldn't have been gay and wouldn't have had to deal with all that comes with it. I know that's not how gay works, but it doesn't change the fact that that is how I felt."

"When did he find out Daddy wasn't his daddy?"

"I think he was about five. I wanted him to know as soon as he could understand. I told him not to tell anyone, and that if he did, he wouldn't get any candy. I don't know what made him not tell anyone as he got older, but he didn't."

"Why didn't you want anyone to know?"

"See, Ivory, you are part of the new school. Back then, they would put a red letter 'W' for 'whore' on your chest and hang you out to dry for just having a baby out of wedlock. Do you know what my parents and family and church and friends would have done to me if they found out I didn't know who my baby's father was? What they would have done if they found out that my husband wasn't his father?"

"No."

"I don't, either. And I wasn't going to find out. Your father and I knew of each other. We lived the same life, ran the same streets, played the same games. We had a few conversations before and flirted with each other. We were no strangers to each other.

"Word had gotten to him about me. That I was… free and enjoying life. He approached me about dating and whatnot. I was straight up with him. I told him that I was four weeks pregnant. I told him that if he married me, he'd get it whenever and wherever he wanted. He married me five days later. I rathered the tongue lashing people gave me for marrying a man so fast than the lashing I would have gotten for getting pregnant out of wedlock and not knowing who my baby's father was.

"Our marriage didn't last because neither one of us was done whoring around. We didn't match each other. He married me for the consistent ass, and I married him to save face. And for the money. Everyone knew that he and his family had money. I thought I could deal with whatever as long as the money kept rolling in. I was wrong. I couldn't.

"To make it clear as day, Curtis is not Curtis, Jr.'s father. I don't know who is, but it's not Curtis. I was pregnant before Curtis and I ever had sex."

"CJ is the one who told me he wasn't his dad, not Jackie. Jackie never confirmed or denied it. She always literally said nothing. I'm not sure if she even knows."

"Oh, she knows. He told me she knows."

"Well, she never said anything to me about it."

"Okay," she said, nonchalantly.

I was there to mend my relationship with her. I wasn't going to push it by trying to mend her relationship with Jackie. I could fight only one battle at a time.

"And you wanted to know if I ever thought about you and if you were a burden. I thought about you all the time. You were not a burden. You were just… built different. I knew that you would make it. You didn't need me for every little thing. You were strong.

"I see now that I should have been better. I see a lot of errors. I can't go back. But I am sorry for it. I will do my best to be better to you. I am all for having a relationship with each other. Are you?"

Tears were streaming down my face. I nodded my head "yes".

"Good." She looked out the window in silence. Emotions, vulnerability, honesty, and talking openly were all new to her, so she was awkward. But she was trying.

I wanted to tell her about how my meeting with CJ went, but I chose not to. I didn't want her to feel as though she had to choose between us. Truth be told, I didn't want my feelings hurt. Lord knows who she would have chosen. She would not have chosen me.

I wondered what her feelings toward CJ were. Was there any animosity since Luna was in the hospital because of him? Did they talk at all? Does Luna see the dead eighteen wheeler's driver's face every time she closes her eye? Was Luna hoping that CJ would get out soon? Would Luna have to testify whenever CJ's court case came up? Did CJ have a court date set, yet?

But those questions were for another day. We sat there in awkward silence for about thirty minutes before I told her I had to go because my ride was waiting outside. We didn't have to talk. We were on our way to being better, and that was enough for me.

Maybe hospitals weren't a dream snatcher as I previously believed. Just maybe it wasn't a place where faith went to die, but a place where faith is restored. Maybe hospitals weren't just for healing the physical being. Hospitals also served as a place to heal the mental state and emotional being. Hospitals healed relationships and restored peace. Even created peace that was never there. Maybe, just maybe, a hospital was the answer to my prayers.

Chapter 28

Ding!

I got to ring the bell! It was my discharge day from the facility. I had completed the program, and that was symbolized by a small ceremony in the dining room. It was more of an individualized plan, and I was finished after two months. Of course they suggested that I continue therapy once I was home. It wasn't a bad suggestion; I just didn't need it. There was nothing else that needed to be done. I had me back.

That day, I wore my daddy's socks to my "graduation". The man loved to shop. When he passed away, he had goo-gobs of clothes! Two color-coordinated walk-in closets were overflowing with fur coats, alligator shoes, suits, ties, dress shirts, and a Chester drawer filled with brand new dress socks, underwear, and sweaters. Jackie offered us all to take what we wanted when he died, and we donated what we didn't want to a shelter that helps out reformed men. Anyway, I kept a few of his dress socks and fedoras for myself. I liked to wear them at times when I was really missing him. My ceremony really had me missing him. Not in a hopeless or helpless way; I just missed him. I wore his rainbow polka dot pair of socks.

My husband, Que, Mychaela, and Jackie came to my ceremony. It stung a bit because when I looked at the other patients, they had tons of people there. But four people are better than none. One person had nobody.

It was extra important for Mychaela to be there because I wanted her to see her mom get help. I wanted her to know that it is okay to not be okay. I wanted her to see her mama do whatever she had to do to be her best. I needed to be a great example and role model in every way, including taking care of my mental health.

She had seen me lose weight, caring for my physical health. She saw me go to church every Sunday and attend the prayer call every Wednesday, taking care of my spiritual health. She saw me regularly go to the doctor, caring for my overall health. She had to see me take care of my mental health, too. Mental health is health. The mind is a part of the body just like the hands, feet, heart, etcetera.

I take that back. Five people were there for my ceremony: my husband, Que, Mychaela, Jackie, and *me*! I count as a person there for my ceremony because I was there for me. I showed up for me.

I was done with CJ. I had no desire to have a relationship with him. He killed my dad. I knew it from the beginning, and I knew for sure since Day 10. I stayed up a few nights contemplating how I would re-present him without evidence to the police as a suspect until my dad came to me in a dream. He told me that I didn't have to do anything because he was already tormenting CJ every day with memories of what he did. He said that CJ hasn't slept in months and that he had no plans of letting up.

Knowing that CJ was in hell was all the peace I needed. I let it go because I knew that Daddy's spirit wouldn't let him go.

I was so grateful to the program. Even the cheesy group sessions we did that made us mock each other so that we all would see how we looked and sounded to the rest of the world. I would've never reached out to my brother and mom had I not admitted myself to the facility. I would've never been honest with myself about the way I felt about my dad. I would've never been honest with myself about anything. I needed therapy, and therapy needed me. I regret nothing.

Chapter 29

"Pastor preached her wig off today, didn't she?!" Charles said to me, sitting on the side of the bed, taking his shoes off. "It felt so good having my wife back in church with me."

I don't know what it is about him taking his shoes off that makes me throb between my thighs. Maybe it's the symbolism of him taking the day's stresses off. The representation of him getting comfortable in my presence. The meaning behind him undressing, feeling safe enough with me to be naked.

Not just naked in the sense of no clothes. But transparent. Allowing me to see him at his weakest. Allowing me access to something no other person has access to.

I straddled him and allowed my hands to roam his physique. It had been a while. One year and nine months to be exact. He had been so patient and understanding. A complete gentleman. But I didn't need a gentleman this day. I needed a beast.

My body was inviting and accepting, and he felt that. There was no hesitation on his end. He returned every emotion and ounce of passion that I delivered. We ached with wanting each other so bad that our desires fought for first place.

Mine won.

I allowed him to enter my mouth, and his soul left his body. He grabbed the back of my head and pushed it up, down, up, down, round and round. He thrust his hips into my throat, pumping harder and harder, slutting me out, and I loved the fuck out of it.

The aching between my lower lips wasn't letting up. I couldn't bare it anymore. I placed his dick inside me and rode him like I was at a rodeo. Wasn't no getting thrown off. I was in it to win it, to endure until the end.

He flipped me over, laid me on my back, and stood up in it. It was the most delicious pain I'd ever experienced. I couldn't dare tell him to let up or stop. I needed everything he was offering.

My walls trembled around his manhood. He exploded into my core. His body collapsed on the side of mine. We cuddled without tears streaming down my face for the first time since my dad went missing.

"This was… whew." He exhaled. "Sorry for the early finale. It's been a while."

"You deserve to last as short and end as soon as you want to. That's the least I could allow. Seriously, Bae. I don't know where Mychaela and I would be without you. You were thrown in to navigate this storm alone. I know this isn't what you signed up for. Thank you for being patient with me. Thank you for loving me when I may have been hard to like. Thank you for being my rock. For lifting me up when I was weak. Thank you for praying with me and for me. Daddy always said I found me a good man when I found you. Daddy was right. Thank you for waiting on me."

"Well, nobody else wanted me, so…"

"Daddy always told me to marry somebody as ugly as him. No competition."

"He also told you to marry rich. One for two ain't bad."

"Can't win 'em all, Charles. I can't win 'em all."

"I did, though. Everything that I prayed for, you are more. There's no one else, Ivory. Just you. I'll wait a year, decade, century, past Jesus' return for you. Time is not an issue as long as I know you're the trophy in the end."

"But what about the girls before me? The one with the bigger booty? The one with the bigger titties? The one with the thicker thighs? The one who became a surgeon? That floozy at church? That big booty dancer chick? They all still want you. What about the women who have approached you in my absence? The ones who were willing to do whatever whenever however?"

"They're all dead to me."

Missing You...

We always believe that we have tomorrow.

We take for granted the present,

believing there'd be no sorrow.

I dialed you several times,

but you never picked up the phone.

I patiently waited for your response,

but God had called you home.

I am heartbroken and saddened

And I don't understand.

But God wanted you by his side

So He reached down and grabbed your hand.

I am thankful to have the memories

And lots of pictures with your beautiful smile.

I will look at them often and that should comfort me for a while.

You are my daddy

The first man I ever loved!

I will miss you and need you to comfort me from above.

Forever Your Bay-beeee,

Ivory

BOOK CLUB QUESTIONS

1. Which character did you dislike the most and why?

2. Why do you think Curtis, Jr. treated Ivory the way he did?

3. If you could add an alternative ending, what would it be?

4. At what point in the book did you know that Ivory's mother and brother were never really dead?

5. While this book surrounds family relationships during a crisis, how important is it to maintain "family" relationships when they are unhealthy?

6. What steps do you use in setting boundaries for your mental health?

7. Considering the state of Ivory and CJ's relationship, do you think people are prone to accept or tolerate toxic personalities and behaviors when it's a family member involved?

8. When Ivory imagined her father returned after being missing, what did you think?

9. Would you have been so forgiving of Ivory's mother?

10. What do you think of Ivory's visit with CJ while he was in prison?

11. Who was your favorite character and why?

12. Was there any part of the story that made you emotional?! If so, which part? Why?

13. What was your favorite part of the story?

14. What was your least favorite part of the story?

15. Before finding out that Ivory's mother and brother were alive, how did you think they died?

16. Was Ivory wrong in her feelings towards her mother and brother? Why? Why not?

17. Could Ivory have tried harder to mend the relationship with CJ?

18. What did you think of Dr. Mable's unconventional therapy style? Would you go to an unconventional therapist? Why? Why not?

19. What part of this book will you always remember?

20. When Luna gave her reason for treating CJ better than Ivory, did you feel less animosity towards Luna?

21. How did you feel about Curtis, Sr. naming CJ after him, knowing he wasn't his son?

22. Should Ivory's parents have told her that CJ wasn't Curtis Sr.'s biological son?

23. Do you think that Ivory and Luna's relationship will get better? To what extent? Do you think it will ever be the mother-daughter relationship that Ivory desires?

THANK YOUS

Woo-hoo! Daddy, I DID IT!!

Thank you to God for your almighty blessings. Thank you for showing me love, giving me strength, and allowing me the words, vision, and wherewithal to write this book.

Thank you to my not-your-ordinary book club EyeCU Reading & Social Network sister circle: Bayyinah Jackson, Monique Woods, Rhena Holmes, Samara Erkard, Satanya Elcan, Stacye Lewis, Tamara Walker, and Tina Smith. I couldn't imagine life without you ladies. God knew what He was doing when he put us together. Together, we've weathered many storms. You ladies challenge me and push me to be great at the same damn time. Samara & Tamara, I don't know if you remember, but about a year ago after one of EyeCU Reading's virtual book discussions, we were the last three left on the call. It was that talk that gave me the confidence I was lacking and catapulted my writing of this story. Thank you for your encouragement and for believing in me when I didn't believe in myself. Who knew that a book club would turn into such a phenomenon? I love you ladies. We are blessed to have one another.

Victoria Christopher Murray and Reshonda Tate Billingsley... I DID IT! Here's my BIG BOOK‼ It was your writing classes, encouragement, and guidance that gave me the push that I needed to put my words on paper. I appreciate you more than words can express.

Christine Paul...Thank you for reminding me age ain't nothing but a number and that you're never too old to pursue your passion.

Joey Getz, Brandon Bingham, Angela Edwards, Sherri Boo, Charles Richard, Melanie Urban, Cheryl Ford, Lief Mason, Martina Duby Liskova, Sarah Andrade, Kara Markham, David Sigel, Grey Allen, Janelle Richardson, Diane Mitchell, Shannon Rose, and Viranel Clerard... You guys have been some of my biggest encouragers. Thank you for letting me bounce ideas off of you. You gave me the push I needed when I didn't think I had it in me.

Daniel Byrd… The man behind the lens! I said I wanted a custom cover and your photography produced just that. Thank you for helping to bring my vision to life. I'm in love with my cover because of you.

It takes a village. Stephanie Fazekas-Hardy, Tanisha Stewart, Ben Burgess Jr., E. Raye Turonek,

Untamed, Sylvia Hubbard-Hutula, Leslie Wright, Sheryl Lister, Lisa Renee Johnson, Debra Owsley, Nakia Plummer, Joan Vassar, and Monica Fontenot-Walters... Thank you all for your encouragement and support.

Angie Ransome Jones, Kena Reshay Williams and Dean Swift, Octavia Grant, and Aja Graves... Your support and guidance is priceless. Thank you for tightening me up. I did it right because of you.

Sister Rhonda Moore...Thank you for always being down for whatever. Although we got off to a late start, having you has been a great comfort. I couldn't imagine life without you.

Beverly Joan Williams, a.k.a. Grand B, thank you for just being you! Thank you for being the greatest other mother that a girl could be blessed with. You have one of the biggest hearts I've ever witnessed. You've always gone above and beyond and loved me and my family as your own. We love and appreciate all that you are.

To my editor Jhordynn, you are the bomb, and your energy is infectious. Throughout the fears and doubts, you were right there pushing me to the finish line. Every time I doubted myself, I could hear you in the back of my head saying, "Do it scared. Just write! Write everything that comes to you. You got this!" Thank you for your guidance because Lawd knows I had no clue as to where to begin.

Tina Smith, someone once told me that timing is everything. When I think back on that 98%, I think, *Look at us NOW!* You an editor and me an author! We're for real for real out here catching dreams. And to reflect on where we started to how far we've come, I couldn't be more proud at this time in my life to call you a friend and see you achieve your dream as a professional editor and business owner of Precise Editing Services. Timing really is everything, and I'm so glad we took the time to get here. Thank you, Colgate for giving my baby the Precise Editing polish-up! I love and appreciate you for all that you do.

Mary Quantavia, my beautiful Goddaughter. Your mom knew what she was doing when she named you Quantavia. I never knew what the name Quantavia meant until I started writing. Quantavia means "a beautiful young lady who strives for nothing but greatness! A beautiful friend and listener". You have definitely lived up to the definition of your name. Your name is as beautiful as you. And as unique as you. Throughout the years, it has been a proud pleasure to watch you blossom into the strong and vibrant young woman that you are today. Your sky has NO LIMIT!

Last but not least...Shannon Harper, thank you for cracking the whip! Unbeknownst to you, your teasing threats stayed in my ear. Here's that book you bullied me into.If there's anyone I forgot, please don't charge it to my heart.

Join our virtual book club: EyeCU Reading & Chatting
https://www.facebook.com/groups/670686289760084/?ref=share_group_link

Follow Author Ebony on FB:
https://www.facebook.com/Author-Ebony-Evans-101181896043076/

Follow EyeCU Reading's fan page: EyeCU Reading & Social Network
https://www.facebook.com/profile.php?id=100063715056766

IG: eyecu_ reading
https://instagram.com/eyecu_reading?igshid=YmMyMTA2M2Y=

ABOUT THE AUTHOR

A Detroit native, Ebony Evans has always had a knack for creating and implementing exciting out-of-the-box ideas. EyeCU Reading & Social Network is a combination of a grand idea fused with one of her dynamic passions…reading.

The loud and proud founder and president of EyeCU Reading & Social Network and EyeCU Reading & Chatting, Ebony Evans is an enthusiastic reader, reviewer, and self-proclaimed "book nerd" at heart! In addition to reading and being a devoted wife and mother, Ebony loves laughing, cooking, dancing, karaoke, and spending time with family. Life has taught Ebony the value of surrounding herself with a close-knit circle of like-minded supportive friends, with whom she reciprocates compassion and that same support.

Ebony has been married since 2000 to her soulmate Michael, and together, they have one fur baby, Lacy, and a high energy and very talented daughter, Essence. Essence's "bigger than life" personality and sleuth of extracurricular activities keep Ebony and Michael very busy and very proud as they watch her grow into a dynamic young adult.

If you would like to connect with Ebony via social media, she would love to hear from you!

FB: Author Ebony Evans
FB Group: EyeCU Reading & Chatting
FB Fanpage: EyeCU Reading & Social Network
Goodreads: Ebony EyeCU Evans
IG: eyecu_ reading

THANK YOU FOR READING! PLEASE LEAVE A REVIEW WHEREVER REVIEWS ARE ACCEPTED.

THE END

Made in the USA
Monee, IL
20 June 2023